Coke Girlz

Romell Tukes

Lock Down Publications and Ca$h Presents
Coke Girlz
A Novel by *Romell Tukes*

Coke Girlz

Lock Down Publications
P.O. Box 944
Stockbridge, Ga 30281
www.lockdownpublications.com

Copyright 2022 Romell Tukes
Coke Girlz

All rights reserved. No part of this book may be reproduced in any form or by electronic or mechanical means, including information storage and retrieval systems without permission in writing from the publisher, except by a reviewer who may quote brief passages in review.
First Edition March 2022
Printed in the United States of America

This is a work of fiction. Names, characters, places, and incidents either are products of the author's imagination or are used fictitiously. Any similarity to actual events or locales or persons, living or dead, is entirely coincidental.

Lock Down Publications
Like our page on Facebook: Lock Down Publications @ www.facebook.com/lockdownpublications.ldp
Book interior design by: **Shawn Walker**
Edited by: **Mia Rucker**

Romell Tukes

Stay Connected with Us!

Text **LOCKDOWN** to 22828 to stay up-to-date with new releases, sneak peaks, contests and more…

Thank you!

Coke Girlz

Submission Guideline.

Submit the first three chapters of your completed manuscript to ldpsubmissions@gmail.com, subject line: Your book's title. The manuscript must be in a .doc file and sent as an attachment. Document should be in Times New Roman, double spaced and in size 12 font. Also, provide your synopsis and full contact information. If sending multiple submissions, they must each be in a separate email.

Have a story but no way to send it electronically? You can still submit to LDP/Ca$h Presents. Send in the first three chapters, written or typed, of your completed manuscript to:

LDP: Submissions Dept
P.O. Box 944
Stockbridge, Ga 30281

DO NOT send original manuscript. Must be a duplicate.

Provide your synopsis and a cover letter containing your full contact information.

Thanks for considering LDP and Ca$h Presents.

Romell Tukes

Acknowledgments

First and foremost, all praises are due to Allah. Thank you to all the loyal readers who have been rocking with me and giving me good feedback. Shout to the town, Yonkers, NY and Peeky, shout to Moreno, CB, Frazier, YB, SG, Lingo, Banger, Spayhoe, and all the real rights. One time for everybody in Atlanta, GA, zone one to zone six, y'all know the vibes. Much love to the South and Midwest, can't forget 'bout the Westcoast, all the good men and queens locked up in state and feds. The only way to be successful in the streets is to leave them. Think outside the box so you won't get trapped in the box. A mistake is only a life lesson. Overcome your own battles with self-knowledge and wisdom. Take the good out the bad in life and keep good energy. Much love to Ca$h and LDP, the game is ours. For any comments or questions you can hit me up on Facebook at Bama Author. Thank you, enjoy.

Coke Girlz

Introduction

In Atlanta, the drug turf was big time. There were a lot of hustlers in the city when Ashanti linked up with her uncle, and the city started to go downhill.

Ashanti started off dancing, looking for a way out, and Buzz gave her a shot that would change her life. Ashanti formed a crew of chicks, divas out for the paper, just like her.

Local drug dealers started to come up missing in the city, and wars started to break out all over the city because of the robberies and killings that Ashanti and her girls were causing.

Jason and Eddy had certain areas on lock, but when a loose lip sank their ship, the after effect would be worse than a storm hitting. Would Ashanti and her divas be ready for what was ahead when shit got crazy and people started to find out the girls were really behind the madness?

Atlanta trap life would never be the same, once the divas take control, because Ashanti, Faith and Elisa weren't the type of bitches to be reckoned with.

Romell Tukes

Coke Girlz

Chapter 1

South Atlanta, GA

South Atlanta High School parking lot was filled with students who were happy it was the last day of high school for all of them.

Today was graduation, and Ashanti was looking around for her sister so they could leave.

Ashanti was one of the baddest bitches in the school. She was brown skinned, with hazel, chink eyes, long thick hair, and perfect curves. At eighteen years old, she stopped traffic.

Most young ladies in the south were very thick at a young age, and Ashanti had been thick in all the right places since she was a kid, so she learned how to deal with attention.

She looked at all the students, shaking her head. She hated the kids in her high school. Since the eighth grade, she had been coming here and had to deal with all the haters.

Her main worry was what she was going to do now that school was out. Ashanti acted like she had a plan to other students, but in reality, she didn't have shit.

"Ashanti," a cute white girl name Melanda shouted, approaching her.

"Hey, Melanda."

"Where's Candra?"

"I have no clue. That's who I'm waiting on." Ashanti took off her graduation cap, sitting it on the trunk of Candra's car.

"Oh, well you looked successful, like a model walking up on the stage. Me and Sarah think you're going to be the most outta everybody," Melanda said.

"I hope so."

"What's your plan?"

"For what?" Ashanti shot back.

"When you leaving here, what's your plan?"

"I'm going to college," Ashanti said, with her country accent.

"Where you going?"

"Miami University," Ashanti lied.

"To take what?"

"Why so many questions?" Ashanti got frustrated.

"Sorry, just hoping we could've landed in the same school, but I'm going to Texas A&M," Melanda said proudly.

"Well, good for you."

"I know right."

"That's your sister." Ashanti pointed toward the school gym where Sarah was waving.

"Yeah, hold this. I'll be right back." Melanda handed Ashanti her purse and ran off.

Ashanti saw her run off, and being the nosy bitch she was, she looked into the purse to see a roll of money.

Ashanti saw one of her nerdy classmates drive by in a Honda truck. "Mell, let me get ride," she asked.

"Sure." Mell was a nerdy white boy, who was smart. She got in the car with him, clutching onto the purse for dear life.

"Where you want me to take you?" Mell looked at her pretty face, trying not to stare.

"You know I live in College Park."

"Oh, yeah," he said nervously, because he tried to stay out of the ghetto parts of town.

Mell came from an upscale family. His dad was a judge and his mom was a cop.

"Thanks."

"What you doing with yourself now?" he asked.

"Why everybody keep asking dumb questions?" she yelled.

"Sorry, but I heard Candra got accepted to go to Spellman College," Mell stated.

"I'm not her."

"So you basically don't have a plan?" he asked, driving through East Point.

"No, I don't," she said.

"Damn."

"How about you, since you asking me a bunch of shit?" She looked between his legs to see a hard-on.

Coke Girlz

"I'm going to police academy in a few weeks. I'ma be a cop. I been took the test." He said.

"Good for you, Mell. Just don't pull me over if you ever see me," she joked.

"I would never. But aye, is that Melanda's purse?" Mell said, looking at the purple Gucci purse, which he'd seen his ex-girl with daily, in her hands.

"Nah, I just got one from my boyfriend, as a gift," she lied good, and he nodded his head.

"Oh, cool. Your boyfriend dropped out last year, didn't he?"

"Yeah."

"He was the school star quarterback on the football team, right?" he asked.

"Yeah."

"What happened?"

"His mom died and his plans changed, for better or worse," she said, thinking about Alex, her boyfriend.

"I think this is you?" Mell pulled up to a corner store in College Park, scared to go any farther.

"Thanks for the ride."

"No problem. I'll see you around, I guess," he said, looking at the goons outside

"Maybe."

"Are you going to that party?"

"No. Bye." she got out the car and walked in the store, passing older goofy niggas.

Ashanti saw Melanda's phone was ringing. She turned it off so she could sell it to the store owner, who bought phones.

11

Romell Tukes

Coke Girlz

Chapter 2

South Atlanta High School

Candra had been talking with her friends for over an hour about all of their future goals and plans for the summer.
"Candra. Candra." Melanda came running up to Candra and two of her friends she'd been hanging with since middle school.
"Yes, Melanda," Candra stopped her conversation about college.
"Have you seen Ashanti?"
"No, I thought she was in the parking lot." Candra looked at her watch, forgetting her sister was trying to go home.
Candra was so happy and excited about finishing school and going to college that she forgot about Ashanti being outside.
Ashanti was anti-social and had no friends, but Candra was different. She was popular, and the smartest chick in the school.
"She was, but when I came back out, she was gone with my purse that I asked her to hold," Melanda said in a panicked voice.
"Do you have your phone?" Candra asked.
"No, but I just called off Sarah's phone and it rang a few times, then it started to go to voicemail," Melanda cried.
"Ok, I am going to get to the bottom of it. Ashanti may have forgot. I am headed home anyway," Candra stated.
"Ok, thank you. Just call Sarah's cell phone. I'll be with her," Melanda said, knowing Candra was going to handle it.
"I have to go. Call me later, y'all, ok?" Candra said leaving.
On her way home, she called Ashanti, but got no answer. She wondered how Ashanti got home, but she didn't put too much thought into it.
Her mom was a correctional official at a jail and wouldn't be home until later, but she knew Alex would be there.
Candra was happy she'd gotten into one of the best colleges in Atlanta called Spellman.
She wanted to become a judge for the city district court, so she planned to take whatever steps that needed to be done.

13

Driving through College Park, she saw hoodlums and thugs all over the place, hustling and doing illegal things.

Living in College Park, she knew a lot of people died out there. She felt sad for people, but she knew everybody had choices.

Her older brother, Jason, who lived with his girlfriend, was a primary example to her. Their mom kicked him out for selling drugs last year because she was against it.

Luckily her younger brother was getting his GED, since he'd recently dropped out of school.

The worst influence in her family was her Uncle Buzz, who was a big-time drug dealer.

They'd never meet their father, but their mom said he was a very bad man, with other kids. That was the most they would get out of her.

Candra pulled up to their house, which was a few blocks up from the projects.

Luckily their mom had a good job so they were able to live in a nice home in a decent area.

Candra parked her Toyota and went inside. She could hear moans coming from Ashanti's room.

"Oh shit, fuck me."

The loud noise made her shake her head and go get a snack.

Ashanti would bring Alex over twice a week when their mom wasn't there.

Candra had sex one-time last year with her boyfriend, but it only lasted two seconds. Her boyfriend, at the time, was a high school jock, just trying to brag about fucking her.

When she heard the rumors in school, she pressed her boyfriend and he laughed in her face.

Candra was embarrassed, but she got even by telling everybody he had a two-inch dick. That rumor affected him so bad that she made him drop out of school.

Alex came out sweating, fully dressed. He gave her a head nod before leaving.

Coke Girlz

Candra walked in Ashanti's room, smelling a sex odor in the air. It wasn't a musk smell, and the scent of cherry was in the air, also.

Ashanti was in her mirror wearing her booty shorts and fixing her hair, while looking at Candra through the mirror.

"What?"

"Nothing."

"I was waiting on you, but you was too busy with your nerd friends that I hate," Ashanti announced.

"They're my friends."

"Of course, but why are you in my fucking room?" Ashanti asked.

"I forgot to ask you, do you have Melanda's purse? She was acting like a bitch over it," Candra said.

"No, I do not. Now bye," Ashanti said, getting up to close the door in her face.

Candra saw the purple Gucci purse on Ashanti's bed and knew her sister couldn't afford a new Gucci handbag.

She knew Ashanti was shiesty but stealing was something she would never think of.

She left Ashanti's room, thinking of the party later that night at a club one of her friends' family had rented out so they could have a graduation party.

***

Later that night, Candra had on a nice red dress she'd stolen from her mom's closet.

She got out of her car that was barely working and saw her two friends waiting on her.

"Y'all here, looking like hookers," Candra said, seeing the short skirts and mini dresses squeezing their curves.

"We trying to catch," one of them said laughing.

"Well, we better enjoy. We only graduate high school one time," Candra said.

"True, let's go party," one of her friends said.

"Where is Ashanti?"

"I don't know, nor care. Let's enjoy ourselves," Candra said, walking in the club to hear Da Baby's song playing through the loudspeaker.

Coke Girlz

Chapter 3

One year later, Atlanta, GA

Ashanti was on stage in Magic City strip club, shaking her ass on the pole, in a pair of lime green thongs, which her ass swallowed. She made her ass clap to the club music, making a few ballers go crazy. Other exotic dancers hung from the ceiling and did a bunch of crazy shit.

She'd been working there for three months and hated it, but she had no choice but to work the pole, to make ends meet for herself.

Last year, when she graduated from high school, she never could have imagined she would be a stripper in the nightclubs in Atlanta.

Her sister went off to college and left her alone in her mom's house, who was forcing her to get a job.

Ashanti still lived with her mom, who thought she worked overnight at a warehouse somewhere in the city.

She felt bad, lying to her mom, but she needed to start stacking money so she could eventually get her own crib with her boyfriend, Alex, who worked a regular nine to five job at a store.

Alex wasn't tripping that she was stripping because she was helping him put clothes on his back. She was the reason he had a new truck.

Ashanti was making over seven bands a night dancing, on a good day. She was loving it, but the only issue was how she was feeling.

Men in the club violated women, grabbing her pussy, slapping her ass, sliding their finger in her pussy or ass.

Every night she had to deal with some type of disrespect, and she hated it.

Her night was done, so she went to get dressed in the locker room that smelled like stank pussy and feet.

Ashanti wondered how the customers didn't smell the strippers' body odor, or the fish smell some of them had.

17

There were two strippers that showed Ashanti the ropes, and she fucked with them, but both women were never there. The two women did mostly private parties and house events. Creamy and Sayla were about their money, and they took a liking to Ashanti. They even gave her the stage name she used, Honey.

Leaving the club, she saw someone waiting outside on her car. When she got closer, she couldn't believe who it was.

"Uncle Buzz," she yelled, hugging her uncle.

"What's up, Mini?" he said, calling his niece the name he'd been calling her since she was a baby.

He called her Mini because she was born tiny. Growing up, she started to blossom quick, too quick.

"I saw you in there, but I ain't know that was you with them big ass gold chains on," she joked.

"I knew that was you, had to close my eyes. I told my crew to, also," he said.

"Sorry, Unc," she giggled.

"It's cool, but how's your mom? She know you dancing?"

"I'm grown now, Uncle Buzz," she shot back.

"You nineteen."

"Yes, grown."

"You know she gonna kill you." Uncle Buzz knew his sister like the back of his hand.

"She will be ok, but what's up with Jason?" she asked.

"He outta town right now," Uncle Buzz said.

"I know what that means."

"He doing big things. You need to get at him. I'm sure he will disapprove of this." He pointed at the club.

"He not finna put no money in these pockets," she said.

"I hear you shawty. But how you pay to get your body done?"

"This all me." she slapped her ass, making it clap.

"Ok, well like, take my number. If this shit don't work, I got another job for you," he said, writing down his number on a piece of paper.

"I don't sell pussy."

"What? Gurl, shut up. I would never ask my niece to do that."

Coke Girlz

"I don't transport drugs neither," she said, knowing he was a man that jacked all trades.

"Just call me, big head," he said, walking off.

She got in her hooptie, thinking about the offer. She knew her uncle was hood rich, but he lived a different type of lifestyle she knew she wasn't ready for.

***

College Park, GA

Ashanti saw her mom's car parked in the driveway. She thought she was doing a double tonight at the jail, but she could see now that was not true.

"Fuck," she said, parking on the sidewalk.

Ashanti knew she couldn't walk through the front door, so she had one choice. She crept to the back of her house and pushed the window to her bedroom open.

She sneaked in her bedroom and went to sleep, preparing for the next day and wondering what job her uncle had for her.

Romell Tukes

Coke Girlz

Chapter 4

Zone 4, Atlanta

"Who was that bad bitch you was talking to?" Eddy said from the passenger seat of his boss' Benz.

"Keep your eyes where they supposed to be, young nigga," Uncle Buzz shot back in defense.

"My bad, shawty."

"That's my niece, Jason's sister," Uncle Buzz said.

"Damn," Eddy said too loud, as Buzz slapped him in the back of his head.

"Jason will kill you if he hear you was looking at her," Buzz said, as he pulled into the West End area.

"Shit, she shaking her ass in a club. The whole city can see."

"That's her business. But check this shit out, I want you to go in Busta spot and see what's up wit my money," Uncle Buzz said, pulling over.

"What apartment he live in?" Eddy said, picking up his pistol.

"2J, I think, and hurry up. It's 3am," Buzz said, playing the J. Cole album and liking his energy.

Buzz was a plug in the Zone 4 area, but he supplied other hoods, too. He also had a lot of enemies all around Atlanta.

He had a strong crew. Jason and Eddy were his enforcers. They played no games and had a few bodies drop throughout the city.

"Don't kill him, just get my money," Uncle Buzz said before Eddy exited the car.

***

Eddy was a young savage, who worked for Buzz. He was broke and homeless when Buzz found him on a late night, about to rob a nigga.

Since that day, Eddy looked up to Buzz and listened to everything Buzz said. He looked up to him like a father figure.

Walking to the apartment Buzz had just told him to go to, Eddy smelled a strong odor of weed. Eddy didn't smoke or drink, so when he smelled weed, he could barely breathe.

He tried the door handle, and as he wished, it opened. He crept inside and saw two men rolling up blunts.

The men didn't see Eddy's black ass until it was too late, and Busta's little brother crashed to the floor from the powerful blow.

"Oh shit." Busta jumped up, dropping the blunt.

"Where Buzz money?"

"Who?"

Eddy slapped Busta in the face with his gun as his little brother woke up. "You got five seconds," Eddy said seriously.

"I only got two bands," Busta said.

"What?"

"I got Buzz in a few days, but all I got is the two thousand," he said, looking at the table.

Eddy took the money off the table and pocketed it all.

Boc.
Boc.
Boc.
Boc.
Boc.
Boc.
Boc.
Boc.
Boc.

Eddy killed Busta and his little brother before rushing out the building to see Buzz starting up the car.

"What the fuck just happened?" Buzz asked.

"Oh, he said he not paying you and he going to kill your bitch ass, so I did you the solid and smoked his hoe ass, shawty."

"Oh yeah? That bitch ass nigga was bumping his gums?" Buzz was mad now.

"Yeah."

"I should go kill his mama." Buzz was on fire.

Coke Girlz

Eddy knew how to get his boss and big homie upset. Eddy never saw Buzz put in work. Jason always did it, or him, so he would do little sneaky shit, knowing his boss was too bitch to do anything if he found out.

"It's cool, big bro," Eddy said as he laughed in his head.

***

Albany, GA

Jason was in a house with two bad bitches, who lived out there and were roommates.

He watched them cook the coke over the stove at 400 degrees. They all wore face masks.

Jason had 14 keys on the table to cook up, plus the brick open on the kitchen counter.

Jason was Ashanti and Candra's brother. He was older, at twenty-five, and a very handsome young man.

He stood six feet, with brown skin complexion, dreads, and tatted up. The women went crazy for him.

Working for his Uncle Buzz was very beneficial, and he was getting a lot of money.

Jason hustled in Stone Mountain, Albany, and the outskirts of Atlanta.

"We got four hours, so hurry up and don't fuck up," Jason slapped both women on their phat asses.

He was having threesomes with them every night. He loved his lifestyle. Money was coming too fast and he was beefing with niggas because of his Uncle. Jason caught a lot of bodies for Buzz's dumb shit, and he believed in Karma.

Romell Tukes

Coke Girlz

Chapter 5

Zone 6, Atlanta

Elisa was on break at her job, tired of working double shifts at the Family Dollar, a local store in the middle of the hood.

Elisa was Ashanti and Candra's cousin, who was on her way to college in a few months, but she needed to stack some money first. She wanted better for herself and family.

Elisa was a sexy red bone. At nineteen years old, she had big plans of becoming a famous author. She had a story to tell but telling the world would be a big step for her.

Only a few people, who were close to her, knew about her lifestyle and could relate to her emotions.

As a kid, Elisa's father was a crackhead, and used to take her away from her mother at the age of eleven through fourteen.

When he used to take her, acting like he was spending time with her, he really used to sell her to other drug dealers.

The sexual abuse went on for years, until her father got killed in the street for a twenty-dollar drug debt.

She kept that a secret because her dad used to tell her that he would kill her.

When he died, she shed tears of joy. At her father's funeral, she took his head and bashed it into the casket.

Months after her dad's death, she had a mental breakdown, which led her into a mental hospital.

That wasn't the only time, she'd had two more breakdowns after that, which almost got her stuck in a mental hospital for a long time.

She realized trying to kill herself wasn't the way, and luckily was able to get her shit together.

Elisa finished high school, and now was waiting to start college.

Boys weren't on her mind, like most 19-year-olds, she was focused on money instead.

Looking at two old couples arguing, she tried not to laugh, but she couldn't help it.

A white Benz pulled into the parking lot with tints, and she wished that was her inside. When the luxury car pulled up on her, she wanted to curse the dude out, until she saw who got out.

"Bitch, you looking like you ready to rob a bitch," Ashanti stated, getting out of the car.

"Oh shit." Elisa was happy to see her first cousin.

Elisa's mom and Ashanti's mom were real sisters, so they grew up together, with their other cousin, Faith.

"What you doing?" Ashanti hugged her.

"Bitch, working."

"You work here?"

"Hell yeah, for now, until I start school," Elisa stated sadly.

"Damn. What time you get off?" Ashanti asked.

"In a few hours."

"Ok. I'ma come pick you up. What time?" Ashanti asked.

"At seven."

"Ok." Ashanti got back in her car, pulling off.

***

At seven o'clock, Ashanti's white Benz was parked in the same place she'd parked earlier. Ashanti loved her cousin, Elisa, and seeing her work at Family Dollar did something to her heart.

She knew Elisa's story. Out of everybody in the family, Elisa had it the worst, so to see her struggling, she felt like she had to do something to help. Even though she was a cold-hearted bitch, she still had a soft spot for family and close friends.

Elisa walked out in old clothes, carrying a no-name purse. Ashanti shook her head. She wasn't rich, but she was making enough money to get fly and drive a luxury car. But she wanted more.

Her back and hips were starting to hurt from sliding up and down a pole, stripping. Elisa climbed in the car, happy to see her favorite cousin.

"It smell good in here," Elisa said, looking around.

Coke Girlz

"What it's supposed to smell like, bitch?" Ashanti laughed, pulling off
"Who car is this?"
"Gurl, don't play."
"This you?" Elisa said in shock.
"I'm getting money."
"What you do?"
"I dance."
Elisa looked at her funny.
"Yeah, bitch, I strip at Magic City on Tuesdays and Sundays," Ashanti said proudly.
"Oh shit. I can't believe that."
"Really? I been dancing," Ashanti said, confirming her statement.
"Damn, if it works for you."
"Don't knock it until you try it," Ashanti said.
"I'm good."
"You good rocking JC Penney shit?" Ashanti got serious.
"I'm not going to degrade myself for pennies."
"I got a better way for you to get a bag. I'll fill you in soon," Ashanti said.
"Ok, as long as it's not dancing on a pole."
"Ok. I got you. Facts," Ashanti said, taking her home, thinking about the idea her uncle approached her with.

Romell Tukes

Coke Girlz

Chapter 6

Zone 1, Atlanta

"I'm sorry," the old white woman said as Faith cleaned her up in her bed with a scrubby and soap.

"Sorry for what?" Faith said, not understanding why her client apologized to her.

In seconds, while cleaning the woman's fat legs, she smelled shit, and automatically knew what it was. The woman had just shitted on herself again.

"Again?" Faith had to change the lady's diaper again.

Faith hated her job doing home health care, but it was how she got paid, and it was ok money.

She was Ashanti and Candra's cousin also, but since they lived in different zones, they barely saw each other.

Faith's brother lived in Alabama, where he was getting money. He wanted her to come, but she loved Atlanta too much to just up and leave.

Her favorite cousin, Candra, had just called her, checking on her and seeing how she was doing.

Faith got done cleaning her client, who was over 300 pounds. She was actually close to four hundred pounds. All she did all day was lay in bed and shit on herself.

It was time for Faith to go home. All she thought about was finding a new side hustle.

Her neighborhood was full of money. She knew a lot of drug addicts, and lately, she was thinking about getting some drugs to sell.

She was sick of the way she was living, but she knew God would bless her soon.

Faith wasn't about to do what other women did in the city, go to a strip club to shake some ass for a few dollars. She had too much respect for herself.

Faith looked good. She was a chocolate, slim chick, with a plump booty and piercings all over her face and body. She was bi-

29

sexual, but she preferred men any day. She just liked to have fun, but had been single for a while now.

***

USP Atlanta

The federal prison was in the heart of East Atlanta and was filled with dangerous prisoners, from all over the world, surviving there prison time.

Megan worked had there for a long time. She had over twenty years in as a correctional officer.

She was one of the baddest females in the building. Prisoners and her coworkers just wanted to taste her.

Megan was five-six, brown skin, with a big phat ass and pretty in the face. She was the mother of Ashanti and Candra.

Raising children of her own was hard, especially having two girls and two boys.

She did a good job, but with Jason in the street hustling, she felt like she could've done a better job with him. But she knew there was only so much a mother could do to raise a man.

"Hi, Mrs. Brown," a prisoner said, walking by her, smelling her scent.

"Hi," she replied, carrying her bag, on her way to start her shift.

"Damn," another inmate said, looking at how her jeans hugged her phat ass.

Megan loved the attention, but she didn't like when inmates masturbated to her. When she walked past their cells, they would have their dicks out.

Working in a federal jail, the spot got crazy sometimes and niggas would wild out.

A few guards she knew had lost their lives on duty by violence from the inmates. There was a few inmates she thought about giving some pussy to, but she had to catch herself

***

Coke Girlz

Zone 1, Atlanta

Mills listened to one of his workers explain how he fucked up 200,000 in a police raid.

"Bruh, I swear the niggas took all dat shit, bro," River said.

"The police?"

"Yeah."

"They left the drugs, though, right?" Mills asked as they stood in a shopping center parking lot.

"I got all the drugs."

"Who was all there?"

"Just me, bro," River said.

"So, nobody else was there is what you telling me, shawty?"

"Nah, I was fucking with a little bitch and they—"

"I thought you just said nobody was there?" Mills caught his lie.

"I mean, ole girl came later, and left," River said.

"You got arrested?"

"Yeah, but I made bail that night," River said as sweat dropped down his head.

"Who bailed you out?"

"My mom," River shot back fast.

"I went to your mom funeral with you two years ago, River. Let's keep it real, my nigga," Mills said.

"I would never play with you or your money, big dawg. You know we go way back. We like family," River said seriously.

"I know. But I'ma call you later. I have to go home," Mills said, walking off to his car.

River took a deep breath, happy his childhood friend let him slide with stealing $200,000.

River was fucked up, getting high off coke and dope.

The two men had known each other for years, since they were kids, but that didn't mean shit to a nigga getting high off drugs.

River got in his car, but he didn't see the gunman with the ski mask approach him from behind until it was too late.

Tatt.
Tatt.
Tatt.
Tatt.
Tatt.
Tatt.
Tatt.
Tatt.
The gunman, who was Mills' little brother, ran off through the lot.

***

Mills pulled off when he saw River collapse from the vicious gunfire.

He knew what River did. He stole from him to get high, but the shit he didn't understand was why his boy didn't keep it real.

Mills knew no man was perfect at all, but to cross him was dangerous.

Mills had his little brother put his lights out because it was broad day light and he didn't want to get his hands dirty at that time.

He had workers and traps all over Atlanta. He was one of the big dope boys in the city.

Mills had a lot of ops, but his number one enemy was Buzz and his crew.

The men had beef for years, but Mills knew Buzz had something up his sleeve because he'd been laying low lately.

Mills had a vicious team of niggas getting money in the city, and Buzz tried to pull up on them so they would cross over to Buzz's team.

Coke Girlz

Chapter 7

Downtown Atlanta

Ashanti had called her uncle last night to see if today would be a good day to meet up to see what business plan he had in mind.

Last night, she'd quit her job, so she was in need of some money. She was also eager to move out of her mom's house.

Her two home girls in the club begged her not to leave, but a nigga slapped her on her ass, and another nigga placed his middle finger in her ass.

She felt violated working in Magic City, so she need to find a new lane, and her uncle was the go-to guy.

Ashanti's boyfriend was acting like a bitch since she'd lost her job, because he was really depending on her.

She hated dead weight, and he was that, and some. If the sex wasn't good, and the love wasn't there, she would have been left.

The Underground Mall was full of shoppers and tourists, but she waited in the food court for her uncle, wondering what he had in mind.

She still needed to help her cousin, Elisa, out. Seeing her work at Family Dollar fucked her head up.

Uncle Buzz was walking towards her in a Givenchy sweat suit, with a pair of shades on, looking fly.

Ashanti couldn't help but laugh at him.

"Ashanti, what's going on, baby girl," he said.

"I'm good."

"Ok. You been thinking about what I been telling you?"

"Nah, of course," she laughed.

"Ok. Talk to me."

"I'm not dancing no more, so I need income," she said.

"This type of work is different, very different."

"What you mean?"

"You gotta turn on your gangsta button."

"I don't even know if I have a gangsta button," she joked.

"What? We all got a G button," he told her.

"What will I have to do?" She had a good idea it was about to get very sticky.

"I'm going to have you set up local drug dealers."

"Huh?" She thought he was tripping when she heard this. "Will this work?'

"If you want to get paid and get out of the shit alive, it's gonna work," he said.

"Who will this person be?"

"Person? You mean how many people?" he said, correcting her.

"I'm no killer."

"I know, but I'ma send a killer with you every time you set some shit up," he said.

"What will I have to do?" she tried to figure it out.

"Get the vic back to his crib."

"Vic?" she asked.

"Yes, victim."

"Can we just kidnap them instead?" she asked.

"I never thought of that," Buzz said, thinking that was a good idea.

"I think that's better."

"But you still have to seduce them or bring them to the shooter. But I think it's easier when you go to their crib where the money and drugs will be," Buzz said.

"Money?"

"Yes. You be splitting everything you get down the middle with the shooter I send you with," Buzz said.

"Oh."

"Be smart. This shit can backfire," Buzz confirmed, giving her a serious look

"What if someone try to rape me, or some wild shit?"

"That's the downside to this shit."

"Damn."

"You got pepper spray?"

"No."

"You better get some," he said.

"Ok."

Coke Girlz

"You sure you still down? I know you will be seeing a lot of money, but sometimes you may have to fuck a nigga, suck some dick, get gang banged to open up your vics," Buzz said.
"Gang banged?"
"You gotta do what you gotta do, Ashanti. You not a little girl no more."
"True, but who will we be getting at first?"
"A nigga from Zone 6 named Kiss," Buzz said, like he'd been doing research.
"Zone 6?"
"Yeah."
"Where at over there?"
"Techwood."
"Damn. It's rough over there," Ashanti stated.
"Will that be an issue?" Buzz asked.
"No. I'm saying, how will I find him?"
"He hangs out at a well-known car wash over there."
"So I bag him?"
"Bag him, or follow him, I don't care. I just need you to get him in a good area and call this number." Buzz wrote down a phone number.
"That easy?"
"Sometimes, but if he want some ass, then give it to him."
"I know." She took the note.
"Call that number. Be safe." Buzz walked off
Ashanti's mind was racing now. She didn't know what she'd just signed up for.

Romell Tukes

Coke Girlz

Chapter 8

Zone 6, Atlanta

Kiss and his crew posted up on the basketball court to watch a summer basketball event. Zone 6 was his turf. He sold dope and weed, and controlled basically everything. He worked for M.L., which was his big homie and close peer. When Kiss came home from prison, M.L. put him on with a few keys, and he never looked back.

There were a few bad bitches on the court today, and he had a few lookers.

"What's up?" Kiss saw a big brown skin chick walk by with a nice ass, and another chick.

"What's up? The sky," Ashanti said.

"You spray," Kiss said.

"Facts." Ashanti saw Kiss' boys look at him, giving him the approval to bag her.

"What's your name, shawty?" Kiss asked, looking at her curves in her jeans.

"Ashanti."

"Like that singer chick?" Kiss' homeboy said.

"Better and wetter," she stated, as everybody looked shocked at how hard she was coming off.

"You sure got a crazy mouth on you, sweetheart. You too young to be talking crazy," Kiss said.

"I can back it up," she said, before walking off.

Kiss stood there amazed. He liked her style.

After the game, Kiss approached Ashanti. He'd been watching her since the game started. He'd lost focus of the game and put her in his vision all day. He had to have her.

"Ayo."

"You still ain't figure out my name yet?"

"My bad, Ashanti."

37

"What you want to talk about?" she said, knowing he was on her body.
"I'm trying to take you to a hotel tonight," he said.
"I look like a hotel bitch?' she said with an attitude.
"Nah, shawty. I want to take you to a nice hotel resort spot," he said.
"Ok, you a baller," Ashanti stated, serious.
"I'm trying to treat a Queen like a Queen."
"Take my number and hit me later," Ashanti said.

***

Zone 3, Atlanta

Alex met up with his girl to get some gas money from her so he could go to work.
Alex worked at Best Buy, but he was trying to get a second job. He knew Ashanti had quit her job, but he still needed her help because he was down bad and late on his car note.
Alex still pushed a new Benz, thanks to his girl. Alex was a handsome young man with a mean sex game, but he was broke.
Ashanti pulled up next to him as he checked his g-shock watch.
"Where you been?" he shouted, seeing her hop out in a low cut outfit, looking good.
"What?"
"I need gas money," he said.
"I don't have money. You know I lost my job," she said.
"So what."
"So what? I don't have it."
"Ok, whatever. I'm out," he said.
"It's like that?" she said, seeing him walk off.

***

Downtown Atlanta

Coke Girlz

Later on that night, Ashanti looked sexy in a white Gucci bodysuit, which she borrowed from her girl and forgot to give back. She pulled up to the most expensive hotel in Atlanta. She always saw the big fancy building, but knew it was out of her league. The hotel was more so a resort with a spa, bar lounge, and suits built for kings and queens.

She called the number her uncle gave her days ago.

"Who dis?' the man answered.

"Ashanti. My uncle told me to call you."

"Oh, ok, where you at?" the man asked.

"Downtown at that fancy hotel near the Underground Mall," she said, looking around.

"Ok, I got you," the man said.

"You don't know how I look?" she said.

"I do."

"Hold on," she said before hanging up.

"Fuck nigga," she said, hanging up the phone.

She got a text from Kiss saying suit 15th floor.

Ashanti took a deep breath and exited her car with her heels on, looking like a snack.

Walking into the hotel, she was amazed at how nice the place was. It was nicer than she thought.

She had butterflies in her stomach. She ain't know what her plan was going to be when she got upstairs.

39

Romell Tukes

Coke Girlz

Chapter 9

Downtown Atlanta

Ashanti made it to the room and knocked on the double doors. Within seconds, Kiss opened the door smiling, looking her up and down, and drinking a bottle of patron.
"What's up, Shawty? Come in sexy." Kiss stared at her perfect breast.
"Hey." Ashanti walked into the spot, looking around and amazed at how the suite looked, which she loved.
"I be coming up here to get a piece of mind."
"I see." she sat her purse on the couch and sat down on the soft leather, looking at her sexy cute toes.
"You got some nice feet, baby gurl," he stated.
"Thanks."
"I'm trying suck dem but let me grab a bottle of wine for you." Kiss walked to the kitchen.
Ashanti hurried up and texted the last number in her call log.
"Please hurry. The 15th floor suite, double doors," she texted the unknown man.
"Red or white wine?" Kiss asked with two bottles in his hand.
"Red please," she said, looking at huge dick print poking through his pants.
"Come out to the terrace. It's a view of the city," Kiss stated.
"Ok." she followed him out to the large balcony, looking back at the door, hoping Kiss left it unlocked.
Ashanti saw a Rolex watch on the table, two diamond chains, and a wad of money.
Outside, she looked at the Atlanta skyline, which was bright and picture perfect. The city view could go on a postcard.
"Come here," Kiss said getting behind her and grabbing her ass, palming it.
"Damn, nigga," she said, moving
"Shut up," Kiss yelled, grabbing the back of her neck.

41

Kiss lifted her dress to see her thongs swallowed between her phat ass cheeks. Kiss pulled his dick out, about to take the pussy. This wasn't the first time he raped a bitch. He was known for getting drunk and doing, shit like trying to take some coochie.

"Stoppp," she yelled as he spread her cheeks.

Ashanti kicked her foot back, kicking him in his nuts.

"Ahhhhhhhhh," Kiss yelled, backing up into the rail half his height.

Ashanti pushed Kiss over the rail. Seeing his body flip off the terrace, she couldn't believe what she just did.

"Oh shit," she screamed, looking over the terrace to see Kiss' body crash into the ground, face first, dead.

Thinking fast, she grabbed the chain, watch, and money off the table before running out.

Opening the door, she ran into Eddy, scaring the shit out of her.

"What da fuck?"

"You good?" he asked, seeing how scared she was.

"You Buzz people?" She was sweating.

"Yeah."

"We have to go." She took his hand and ran back inside, forgetting her purse.

"What you do, and where is dude at?" Eddy asked as she ran out the crib with him in tow.

"Shut up and just come on." She ran down the stairs in heels.

Eddy was lost, but he followed her lead and made it outside to see people surrounding a dead man lying in a puddle of blood.

"What the fuck?" Eddy said as Ashanti told him to come on, trying to get away from the small crowd.

Inside her car, she hit the push to start button and pulled off.

"Oh my fucking god," she talked to herself, forgetting Eddy was in the car.

"What happened?"

"I think I killed him."

"You think?" Eddy put two and two together.

"He tried to rape me," she said, about to cry.

Coke Girlz

"That's what Kiss do," Eddy laughed, knowing Kiss was a vicious pussy taker.

"What's so fucking funny?" she asked with an attitude.

"Nothing. I'm not laughing at you, but my car is back there."

"Get it tomorrow. I'm not going nowhere near there," she stated.

"Ok, killer," he joked.

Ashanti stopped at a red light and gave him a dirty look.

"You really a comedian," she told him, seeing her hands were still shaking.

"Gotta get the best out a bad situation. But you can drop me off in Zone 3."

"My pleasure," she said.

Ashanti couldn't get the picture out of her head of how she killed Kiss by mistake.

43

Romell Tukes

Coke Girlz

Chapter 10

College Park, Georgia

The next morning, Ashanti woke up to a ton of missed calls, mostly from her Uncle Buzz and her cousins.

She'd woken up out of her sleep five times last night, thinking about what happened to Kiss.

Ashanti had never killed a nigga, but it made her feel strong and like a boss bitch. She loved the feeling.

Coming so close to being raped, her body felt abused and violated, like she was still dancing in the strip club.

"Ashanti?" her mom yelled outside her door.

"Come in, mom."

"Hey, baby, how was work?" her mom asked, dressed in her job uniform.

"Good, but I recently quit," she said

"You had a good job, baby, but I'll tell you now, you won't be laying up in this damn house without a job. Believe that shit." her mom slammed the door and left the house.

Ashanti shook her head. She saw Alex calling. She really didn't feel like dealing with him today, but she picked up anyway.

"Yes, Alex."

"Hey, baby."

"What do you want, Alex? I don't have no money."

"Don't do me like that, baby. I miss you. I want to see you later and eat that kitty cat," he said, making her smile.

Ashanti loved his dick and head game. He was out of this world with the sex game

"I'll call you later, baby."

"Ok. I'm going to work. I love you," Alex said.

"Love you, too," she said.

Alex was the only man who had her heart. She hated him and loved him at the same time.

She called her uncle so she could tell him what happened.

"Niece," Buzz answered.

"You set me up," she said, putting the phone on speaker and getting dressed.

"What?"

"He tried to rape me," she shot back quickly.

"What? Hold on. Meet me at the park, near the store, near your crib. Try not to talk on the phone," Buzz said before hanging up the phone.

Ashanti had a piece of her mind to give her uncle. She looked at the wad of money she'd got from Kiss and started to count it.

The amount came up to $8,000, all in blue faces. She looked at the jewelry on the dresser, and she knew she was about to cash out.

***

Buzz drove through College Park, thinking about the news he'd heard about Kiss.

Hearing he got tossed off a building made him happy. One person on his list X off.

Eddy said she handled herself well, like a real gangster. When he asked where he was, Eddy told him he was waiting for Ashanti to open up the door for a few minutes before she came.

He knew his niece would come in handy for what he had in mind. But if she had a bigger crew, he could have them take out all of his competition.

Pulling into the parking lot, he saw Ashanti standing in front of her Benz, in a purple outfit. He couldn't lie to himself, if she wasn't blood, he would have been put pipe to her sexy ass.

"Ashanti." he climbed out his BMW sedan big body. "Slow down."

"That nigga tried to take some coochie. You knew he was a creep ass nigga, Buzz."

"My bad. But I heard you did a good job," he said.

Chapter 11

Stone Mountain, Georgia

Jason pulled over when he saw one of his ex-girls standing at a bus stop, looking good in a mini denim dress.

He heard Jamaya was now fucking with one of his rivals, so he really pulled over to pick her brain.

"Jamaya," he yelled, seeing her take her earbuds out of her ear.

Jamaya was mixed, black and white, with a petite body and a pretty face.

"Jason," she smiled.

"You need a ride?"

"Yeah."

"Hop in," he told her, moving a Louis Vuitton backpack full of money out of the passenger seat.

"Where you been at, Jason? I hear you doing big shit out here," she said, looking at his wrist.

"I been good, Jamaya, doing me. But what's been going on with you and Durk?" Jason tried to cut into her, knowing she talked a lot and would give a nigga's blueprint without them even knowing.

"Me and Durk not even together no more," she sucked her teeth.

"What happened?" he acted as if he really cared.

"He was fucking a bunch of stripper bitches and got one pregnant," Jamaya stated with a bit of anger in her voice.

"Damn, shawty," Jason replied, driving through Stone Mountain, up the deep, long hills.

"That's not the worst part," she said, shaking her head, about to cry.

"Nah?"

"This nigga, Durk, gave me three STDs, and one of them is herpes." She had tears in her eyes.

"Herpes?" he said in shock.

"Yeah."

"They don't even got no shit for that, huh?" he asked.

"No, nigga. Durk violated me. I hate that nigga, and he used to talk about you all the time," she said.

"Me?" Jason played dumb.

"Yeah. He used to say he gonna have niggas kill you and rob you. He was really on sum hating shit," Jamaya said, playing on her iPhone.

"That's crazy. He used to be my boy," Jason lied.

"He a snake, Jason."

"I see, but where you going?" he asked ready to drop her off.

"I was going to work at the supermarket. But I want to go to your place and give you what you be missing out on," she said, licking her lips.

"I'll have to get up with you on that. I have to go check on some shit," he stated.

"When can we get together? You know how my head game is, and what this pussy hitting on."

"I know, but I'll call you," he said, pulling over at the supermarket.

"It's like that?"

"I'm just busy today. I'll call you," he said.

"Ok. But I miss you, and still love you," she stated.

"I know," he said as she got out.

Jason saw a few missed calls from Ashanti, his favorite sister. She told him to come pick her up so they could go out to eat, something they did a lot.

He knew Durk was plotting some shit, but he was glad she'd just exposed his hand. Jason had a lot of enemies in the city, but Durk was at the bottom of his bucket list, until now.

Jason had to come up with a plan to handle Durk, soon. It was nothing to drop fifty bands on a nigga's head, and he knew that may be his choice of play.

***

College Park, Georgia

Coke Girlz

Ashanti came outside on this beautiful day in some designer shorts and a tank top, with sandals letting her manicured toes show. She waited on Jason to pull up, so they could go out to talk and chill. These days, she barely saw him because he was running through the Stone Mountain area.

Ashanti got an apartment down the street from her mother's crib. She moved in two days after having a big argument with her mom.

The death of Kiss had been all over the news since his death. She always felt a weird flip in her stomach, hearing his name, because she had a strong guilty conscious.

She sold the jewelry to a pawn shop on Ben Hill, near her hood. With the money, she rented an apartment and paid off her car note. Ashanti gave Alex some money, also, after he ate her pussy for two hours last night.

Alex wanted to move into her apartment, but she told him it was her brother's crib that she was living at. And he believed it.

Jason pulled up and beeped the horn, as if she didn't see him.

"Damn, nigga, you had to beep the horn?" she said, climbing in as he looked her up and down.

"Bitch, next time you get in my fucking car, put some clothes on. Out her looking like you about to slide down the hoe stroll on Bufford Highway," he joked with her.

"Boy, please."

"I thought you was at mommy house." He pulled off, leaving his old neighborhood.

"I moved out."

"You what?" Jason asked, shocked because Ashanti and their mom were always close.

"What the fuck went wrong?" Jason said, beeping his horn at a crackhead who showed him the game growing up, before drugs snatched his soul.

"I quit dancing and picked up a new side hustle," she told him.

"You quit dancing? I told that shit wasn't the vibe. You too pretty and smart to be shaking your ass on some dirty pole."

"Yeah."

"You told her you worked at a club?"

"I'm not dumb, bro. I ain't tell her all dat shit, but she wanted money I ain't have at the moment," Ashanti said.

"How come you ain't call me?" he asked.

"Because I just got a new side hustle."

"What, you clean toilets in shits?" he joked.

"No, asshole, I worked with Uncle Buzz."

"You work with who?" Jason shouted, hoping he heard wrong.

"I got something going on with Uncle Buzz. He helping me out," she said.

"Helping you how?"

"You can't tell nobody, Jason. And I need you to stay out of this, please," she begged. "I be setting niggas up for him," she admitted.

"You fucking joking? That shit will get you killed out here in Atlanta," he said, pulling into Justin's.

"I'm not the one killing them. He got people for that," she said.

"Buzz got a lot of beef in the streets. Ashanti, you have to be smart because if something happens to you, I'm gonna be going crazy," he said.

"Don't worry. It's cool. And I got some chicks from the club that I'ma holla at to get in the mix."

When she said that, a plan went off in Jason's head like a lightbulb.

"Oh, so you about to form a crew of vicious grimy bitches?" he said, seeing her smirk.

"That's a good idea. But I will be honest, the first nigga I killed, kinda fucked me up. I haven't slept since," she said.

"Damn, you already killed a nigga?"

"Not really. Well, I pushed him, after he tried to rape me, and he went over the roof of the hotel," she stated.

"Hold on. You talking about Kiss?" he said, walking into the restaurant.

"Yeah."

"Wow. You know that's going to come back?" he said.

"Fuck it."

Coke Girlz

"I'm with you," he said as they enjoyed lunch.

Romell Tukes

Coke Girlz

Chapter 12

Downtown Atlanta

Ashanti came out to the Trap Museum, which was one of the new hangout spots in the city. She came to get up with Faith and Elisa, to see where their heads were at because she had a plan that could work.

She found it a waste to be a broke bad bitch with nothing, except a nice car and a few designer outfits.

Now, with her own crib and bills that needed to be paid, she was motivated to get to a big bag. The plan she came up with would make anybody laugh in her face, but she was confident it could happen.

Elisa and Faith both walked into the place together, wearing regular attire, walking through the crowd.

"Hey, gurl, what's up?" Elisa said, seeing a seat on the wall where nobody was at.

"Y'all bitches look tired," Ashanti joked, putting her purse down.

"Walk in my shoes for a day," Faith said, sucking her teeth and rolling her eyes.

"Thanks for coming, but I asked the both of you to come here for a reason," Ashanti stated.

"I hope so because I took an Uber out here with money I don't have." Elisa didn't appreciate spending her own money.

"I got a way for us to get some real money out here."

"Bitch, I'm not shaking my ass on a pole," Elisa said.

"Or scamming," Faith added.

"I know four Africans who just got some fed time from scamming," Elisa said.

"Will you bitches just listen? Damn. My uncle and brother gonna have us set up big time dope boys," Ashanti said, looking at the sour look on their faces.

"Buzz and Jason?" Faith asked, as if she knew for a fact it was them. Faith knew Buzz and Jason were the shady type to try to set niggas up.

"Yeah." Ashanti saw the concerned looks on their faces.

"Set niggas up?" Elisa repeated.

"Yes." Ashanti could tell they were both nervous.

"What happens after that?"

"We build a crew and take over the drug game," she said nonchalantly.

"You joking?" Faith laughed.

"Nah, sis. I'm serious as a heart attack," Ashanti said.

"Hold up. You think we gonna take over Atlanta's drug trade?" Faith asked.

"Bitch, you crazy," Elisa said.

"How all dese goofy ass niggas out cha getting money, why can't we run shit?" Ashanti made a point.

"We can't just rob and kill these niggas without shit backfiring on us, Ashanti," Faith stated.

"This is why we build a team of hitters, trained to go for us." Ashanti had it all figured out. She just needed her girls to get on board.

"I'm not trying to fuck no nigga, just to butter him up so we can rob him and shit." Elisa got serious about that.

"You may have to fuck or suck some dick here and there," Ashanti said, as if it was nothing.

"I'm not into that shit," Elisa stated, not feeling the idea anymore."

"Elisa, you might have to get down and dirty from time to time," Faith agreed with Ashanti.

"So, you down with this shit?" Elisa asked Faith.

"Elisa, I need the money. I'm sorry," Faith shrugged her shoulders.

"Ok, but I am telling you, straight up, I'm not for the dumb shit. I'll kill one of these niggas," Elisa added.

"We good. Let's get to this bag then," Ashanti said.

"What's the plan?" Elisa said.

Coke Girlz

"Let me holla at a few dancers and see what's up. We could use my two home-girls," Ashanti stated.

"More people?" Faith didn't like the sound of that.

"I'll need these two chicks," Ashanti stated.

"Who?" Elisa asked

"Don't worry. We in good hands," Ashanti said.

"I hope so," Faith said seriously, not liking the idea of bringing more people into their dealings because she saw a lot shit could go wrong after that.

"I'll need people we can use as bait and screeners to help us rock these niggas to sleep," Ashanti told them.

"Damn, bitch. What you on, some mastermind shit?" Faith asked.

"Nah, I just got a plan that's going to get us rich," Ashanti smiled.

"I'm down for that," Elisa said.

"Me too, bitch." Faith was excited about the arrangement.

All three women left with a goal and plan on their agenda, for the time being.

Romell Tukes

Coke Girlz

Chapter 13

Magic City, Atlanta

Ashanti came out to her old job to throw money and flex on some of her old co-workers. She was really looking for Cream and Sayla to hit the stage, so she could pull up on them.

The money she was tossing was from the jewelry she'd pawned from the Kiss robbery.

She nodded her head to the music, seeing Cream and Sayla both hit the stage and start twerking. Cream climbed the pole all the way to the top. She locked her legs around the pole and slid all the way down. Cream's phat pussy was exposed, showing the crowd.

Sayla was working the floor, pussy popping while doing all types of handstand dances.

Ashanti cheered on her girls as they had the crowd going up. After the women turned up on stage, they went to the back, after picking up their money off the stage.

Ashanti went to the back and saw a few women she use to dance with during her time there.

"Ashanti," a few women yelled, acting happy to see her. But when she'd stopped coming to work, they were talking bad about her.

"What y'all bitches doing?" Ashanti said, smelling perfume mixed with pussy musk.

"Getting money," Cream shouted, happy to see her girl.

"I can tell. But what's with y'all?" Ashanti sat down and asked Cream and Sayla, who were both getting dressed and ready to leave.

"Bout to go hit this private party for some nigga named Durk," Sayla said, applying lip gloss to her thick lips.

Ashanti didn't say a word as the name clicked in her head. It was the same dude her brother was telling her about.

"Durk?" Ashanti stated.

"Yeah. He from Stone Mountain, and I heard he getting to a bag, gurl, a big bag," Cream said, jumping up and down to put her jeans on.

57

"Oh, well I need to talk to y'all about some money moves," Ashanti said as she lowered her voice, knowing chicks were nosey and eaves dropping.
"Yo, money talk," Sayla said. She was surprised.
"Yeah, I'll meet y'all dirty bitches outside." Ashanti got up and went out front

Cream and Sayla looked at each other, knowing Ashanti was on to something.

Cream was a short, thick, southern girl, with a mulatto mix complexion. Her dad was white and mom black.

Sayla was African, and one of the baddest chicks in the club. She was dark, tatted up, and slim, with a nice round ass.

Both women were from Zone 3, the Pittsburg area. They were close friends, who lived together. They danced to get money, but they both had dreams and goals they wanted to achieve in life. Stripping was only temporary.

Outside Ashanti waited for them by their cars. Both women had Audi A8s in different colors.

Cream had an all-white Audi, and Sayla had a candy apple Audi, with twenty-two-inch rims on it.

"Ashanti, this better be good because I normally come out and get the fuck away from here before them stalking as niggas come out," Sayla stated, looking in her purse for a Newport to smoke.

"I need y'all on my team. Me and two of my cousins are robbing the big dope boys in the city and taking over their hoods. We gonna flood it with product, and once I find a steady plug, we can do big things," Ashanti stated, as both of them began to crack up laughing.

"What hood movies you been watching, bitch?" Cream said laughing.

"Movies? That bitch must have been reading one of them gangsta books by that kid, Romell Tukes," Sayla said.

"Girl, he got some good books, and he cute," Cream shot back.

"I'm serious. I really need y'all," Ashanti sounded thirsty.

"You really think Atlanta niggas dumb enough to let strippers get too close to them?" Sayla asked, feeling as if her plan was a bad idea.

Coke Girlz

"I think you tripping," Cream said.

"Do you know how much money we can make?" Ashanti tried to work her gift of gab, but it wasn't working.

"I don't know," Cream said.

"Me either. I'ma sleep on it, but we got to go. I'll call you," Sayla said, getting in her car before tossing her cigarette.

Ashanti watched both women pull off into the dark Atlanta streets, as she came up with a quick plan.

Romell Tukes

Coke Girlz

Chapter 14

Stone Mountain, Georgia

Durk's birthday was turned all the way up. He had strippers everywhere, and a gang of niggas from all over the city of Atlanta. He rented a penthouse suite in the city of Atlanta. Today he was turning twenty-seven years old, so he had a ball.
There were all types of drugs all over the place, and he was high off pills and lean.
Durk was doing big things in the streets. He had a lot of weight moving through the streets of Stone Mountain. Durk's plug was a nigga named DJ from Zone 1, and he was a connected man.
Being young and running up a check, all Durk knew was, in life, you either had to hustle or go against the grain.
The living room was where all the action was taking place. Strippers were clapping their ass everywhere, but two dancers stood out to him.
"Aye, shawty, come here," Durk yelled to the thick woman who came his way with her friend.
"Hey, birthday boy," Cream said.
"I see you brought your friend," he said over the loud music, looking at Sayla in her one piece thong, showing her bald pussy.
"We come here for you," Cream said, grinding on his lap, feeling his hardened cock.
"How about we slide to my crib, a few blocks away? I got a condo we can chill at," Durk said, trying to keep his eyes from closing.
"We down for a good time," Sayla said, rubbing his chains before grabbing their coats.
"Let's roll, shawty." Durk got up and made his way through the crowd, seeing his little brother, Muzzle, approach him with a snow bunny, who was naked and high on coke.
"Where you going, bruh?" Muzzle asked him, looking at the two sexy women with Durk. One of them looked familiar, but he couldn't think back far enough to where he knew her from.

61

"I'm enjoying my night," Durk grabbed Cream and Sayla's hands, leaving the penthouse.

In the elevator, Durk had both women under his arm, feeling like a real pimp.

"You wanna watch us play, daddy?" Cream said, grabbing Sayla's face and kissing her passionately. Cream gave her a long kiss, while sticking a finger into her pussy.

"Uhmmmmmmmm," Sayla moaned as Cream's finger went deep into her tight kitty cat.

"Oh yeah, we finna turn up. I got Molly and coke for you both," Durk said as the elevator stopped at the garage level of the hotel.

"Where's your car?" Cream asked him. Her and Sayla's cars were parked up the street. They didn't want their client to know what they were driving.

Working in the strip clubs and having sex on the side for cash could bring the true stalker out of a real street nigga, if the pussy was good.

"Cadillac truck with the rims." Durk pointed to the white, big SUV, sitting on twenty-four inch rims.

"Ok," Sayla said.

"You drive?" Durk handed Cream the keys, looking at Sayla's phat lips and having a different plan for her.

Getting in the SUV, Durk and Sayla got in the backseat. Cream pulled off and Sayla wasted no time in performing oral sex on Durk. She already had his penis in her mouth, sucking the tip, going up and down. Her phat lips sucked the skin off his pole, and he loved every bit of it.

Durk couldn't keep up with her deep throating him while moaning, making him bust his nut faster.

When he came, she caught all of it, and then spit out the window. They drove down a block full of big buildings.

"Park right here. That's my condo across the street," Durk said to Cream. She pulled over and turned off the car, laughing at how fast her girl made his weak ass cum.

Coke Girlz

"Where your apartment, daddy?" Sayla asked, feeling the breeze under her coat because she only had on a pair of thongs under it.

"1H, baby gurl," Durk said, entering his condo building.

Inside his crib, they were both surprised at how clean and polished it was inside. There was expensive shit all over the place. The rugs were mink, tables were designer, and the furniture was made in a foreign country.

"You hooked this shit up," Cream said, looking around.

"Have a seat. I'ma go take a piss, ok? Be ready for when I get back. I got a dildo I want y'all to fuck me with," Durk said.

"You mean fuck us with it, right?" Cream thought she should correct him.

"No. I want y'all to use it on me, baby gurl," he said, walking off.

"Oh, hell nawl. This nigga tripping. Bitch, I'm ready to go," Cream said.

"Me too." Shayla couldn't believe she'd just sucked his gay cock. When both women turned to leave, Ashanti bum rushed the door with a gun out.

"Oh my God." Cream was scared to death.

"Shhh. Where is he?" Ashanti asked.

"Back," Sayla said, hearing a toilet flush.

Ashanti had been following them since they left Magic City. She was going to get Durk now. She made her way to the back to see Durk coming out of the bathroom in the hallway.

"Don't move again. Where is the shit?" Ashanti asked, seeing Durk trying to get a good look at her.

"Who dat?"

"Where is the money and drugs?" Ashanti asked again.

"You got me fucked up, shawty." he walked towards her.

Boc.
Boc.
Boc.

"Ahhhhh, bitch," Durk yelled in pain, dropping to the floor.

63

"I told your bitch ass not to move. Now where the fuck is the money?" she asked, seeing blood leaking from his arm and shoulder.

"It's all in the safe, under the bed. The code is 7-19-4, just don't shoot me no more," Durk cried on the floor.

"Cream and Sayla, make sure this hoe ass nigga don't move," she told both women, who were rushing to her aid.

Ashanti gave the gun to Cream because she knew Cream would shoot before Sayla would. Ashanti ran to the room in heels and searched under the bed until she found the safe.

"7-19-4," Ashanti said to herself as she turned the combination lock. When she unlocked it, she pulled it open to see stacks of blue face bills in rubber bands. Ashanti took the money and shot Durk in the head, before leaving with Cream and Sayla.

Chapter 15

Downtown Atlanta

The waffle house was like an after-hour spot in the city. Everybody would hit the waffle house after the club scenes, or if a person had the munchies.

Ashanti sat across from both women, eating her waffles and chicken as if nothing just happened.

She lifted her head up to see Cream and Sayla a little shaken up about what just took place.

"Y'all bitches good?" asked Ashanti, taking them out of their daydream.

"Yeah," Cream said, shrugging her shoulders with her hands in her lap because they were still shaking.

"What was that about back there? Ashanti, you ain't even tell us you was coming," Sayla stated.

"Was I supposed to?" Ashanti shot back, looking at both of them.

"I mean, damn, you could have told us you was going to kill him," Cream added her thoughts.

"I'm sorry about that part," Ashanti said.

"Did you really have to do all dat to dude?" Sayla asked.

"Yes because if he would've come back, then we all would have been dead, so I did it for us," Ashanti said.

Since she was a kid, Ashanti's best trait had been her manipulation skills and her smile, which she used for bad and good.

"I guess you right," Cream told the chick she saw grow overnight. When she and Sayla took Ashanti under their wing, they had no clue she had this side to her.

"Do we get any of that money you took?" Sayla had been thinking about the bag of money she saw Ashanti with since they left Durk's condo.

"Did you put in any work?" Ashanti caught her off guard.

"No, but I kinda thought we had an agreement," Sayla stated.

"I don't recall an agreement. I just recall you telling me you'd sleep on it," Ashanti smiled, playing the game.

"Well, can we re-discuss the agreement we had in the club because I want to get down?" Cream said.

"I'm trying to get down too." Sayla needed some extra money so this was the perfect opportunity.

"So y'all with it?" Ashanti said.

"Hell yeah," Cream said.

"I'm trying to get a bag, bitch, so I'ma do whatever need to be done, even if I gotta cut a nigga dick off,' Sayla stated.

"When do we start and what do you want us to do?" Cream asked.

"Just wait on my call, I got y'all," Ashanti said.

"Well, since you got us, do we get some of that money you made tonight?" Sayla had one thing on her mind, and that was cash.

"I'll see what I can do," Ashanti replied.

"Ok," Cream smiled, bouncing in her chair.

"We about to get paid," Sayla said loudly, seeing a few niggas look at her like she was crazy.

"What y'all looking at?" Cream yelled to everybody looking at her best friend.

Ashanti shook her head, happy to have two new troopers on her team. Now she needed some victims to get at.

***

Stone Mountain, Georgia

Jason woke up to the news of Durk's death. He couldn't believe it because he was just talking to his sister about it.

When he heard he got shot on his birthday, in the condo he had downtown, he knew somebody close to Durk had to do it, but he wished it was him. He knew Ashanti couldn't have completed the job that fast and so smoothly, so he knew someone else answered his wishes.

Coke Girlz

Now Stone Mountain was a free for all, open season, and he planned to take over. But there were still a few hustlers he planned to cross out to get to the top.

There was a loud knock at the door, which made him jump up. He saw Ashanti standing outside through the peephole, with a designer bag in her hand.

"Damn, why you banging like twelve?" Jason opened the door for her.

"What? Boy, bye." She closed the door.

"What you want, anyway? I gotta go."

"I killed Durk last night, and robbed him," she said nonchalantly.

"You did that?" Jason couldn't believe she killed him.

"Yeah, and I need you to set up more niggas. Give me a name and location."

"I got you," Jason was still shocked by how vicious she was.

"Thank you, loser. I gotta go," Ashanti said, leaving.

Romell Tukes

Coke Girlz

Chapter 16

Southside, Atlanta

Alex drove his little brother, Style, to East Point because he didn't have a car.

Alex and Style were like day and night. Even though Style was a year younger than Alex, he had his mind right and his affairs in order.

Style had his own crib and he'd been moving pounds of weed and pills because he didn't have a plug on coke, which was a big thing where he trapped at.

Style sold drugs in Zone 3 and East Point. He was cripping with his crew. They were starting to make a name for themselves in the city.

"You still living off that bad bitch?" Style said, moving his gun out of his lower back and placing it on his hip.

"Style, I know you ain't got a gun on you," Alex said in a panicked voice.

"Nigga, stop crying and drive." Style laughed at how scary his brother was.

"When you gonna leave the streets alone? The feds just hit your boy, YBN Lucci, last week, and twenty of his men," Alex said, rolling up his windows so his AC could blow in the car.

"Shit happens, playboy, and death comes with the game," Style said, knowing what it was when he signed up for the shit.

"I was at work and I heard some people talking about you," Alex told him.

"What they say?"

"How you killed a few niggas in Zone 4. Bro, you gotta be smart. These niggas not playing fair out here. I heard you killed a nigga in broad day, shawty."

"I don't know what you talking about, bro," Style lied because he knew exactly what he was talking about. Style killed a man who owed him five hundred dollars. When he caught up to him, he shot him five times in the chest, killing him.

69

"Whatever, this where you going?" Alex pulled over to an apartment building. "Good looks, bruh. Call me." Style got out of the car and disappeared into the building.

Alex had to go to work. He had spent the night with Ashanti at his crib, but he realized she'd been acting funny lately. He barely saw her these days. He had a feeling she was cheating or being on some sneaky shit.

***

Clark University, Atlanta

Candra had just gotten out of class. She had exams and had been studying for a week straight.

She'd barely been getting any sleep, due to hours of studying at all hours of the night. She would take naps, and then wake up and study until she fell asleep.

Her roommate was a party girl. She didn't know how Candra did it. Luckily, it was easy to pass her classes because, unlike Candra, she was having sexual relationships wit two of her teachers.

Candra loved college, but she disliked the students because they didn't take education seriously. They just wanted to party.

Her next class wasn't for an hour, so she planned to meet up with a few nerds to help with a program the school had to offer.

When Ashanti told her she was stripping, Candra couldn't believe it. She knew her sister had potential to be something bigger.

Candra checked her social media page, seeing a few dudes hit her in the DM, but she wasn't interested in relationships right now.

"Candra," a white guy yelled.

"There she go, the smartest girl in school," a nerdy chick in a study room said smiling.

"Hey, let's get this started. I have an hour before my next class," Candra said, putting her bags on the round table

***

Coke Girlz

Downtown, Atlanta

Faith and one of her longtime girlfriends went to Applebee's to get something to eat and catch up.

The whole time there, she saw a handsome, light skin nigga staring at her while he was on a dinner date with a thick, cute, brown chick with bad edges.

"Girl, he all over you," Christian said, taking a sip of her drink.

"I can tell. He cute though." Faith zoomed in on his jewelry and attire.

Since the crew formed, she'd been thirsty to get a victim, and she'd just found her first play.

Faith wrote her number on a piece of napkin and asked the waiter to slide it to the handsome nigga rocking all the jewelry.

She saw when the waiter handed the man the stack of napkins with the number and winked at Faith, while his girl looked at herself in the mirror.

Romell Tukes

Coke Girlz

Chapter 17

Zone 4, Atlanta

Eddy lived with his aunty, for the time being, until he got enough paper to get his own spot. Living with his Aunty Liz was rough. She got high and couldn't be trusted.

His aunty took him in years ago, when his dad got killed and his mom went to prison for a murder. Eddy's mom was a drug dealer. She was getting big money. Even while pregnant with him and his sister, she was still trapping hard.

One thing he respected about his mom was she took care of her kids, no matter what she did or had to do. When he has nine years old, he saw his mom get robbed at gunpoint. Four men ran in their home and tried to rob her, but they only got ten thousand.

A week later, Eddy's mom saw one of the men who robbed her in front of a store, and she killed the man in broad daylight, in front of five witnesses. When his mom got sentenced to life in prison, his aunty took him out of foster care and raised him. Everything went downhill when his aunty started fucking with a nigga, who was recently home from prison.

Liz started smoking crack and everything went downhill. Eddy raised himself in the streets of Atlanta. Luckily, he'd met Buzz, and his life changed. Now he was running through each zone, killing and robbing for Buzz, who let Eddy run the show. Being around Buzz for so long, he watched and learned. One thing he took from Buzz was how to be a snake and lion in the game.

Buzz showed him the game, and he took off with the craft of killing and moving keys. Since meeting Ashanti, he'd taken a liking to her, but he knew Atlanta chicks couldn't be trusted at all. Eddy was cool with her brother, Jason, so trying to get at her would make him feel weird. He had a mutual respect for her brother.

Jason was a killer, just like him. Later that day, he had a meeting across town to discuss some things with Jason and Buzz.

Eddy heard his aunty in the kitchen, yelling and cursing as she always did. He'd been had enough money to move, but he did not want to leave his aunty there. Even though Liz was a headache, he still remembered all the good she did for him, by taking him in. He locked his room door and walked into his closet, moving clothes and shoe boxes to get to his safe. Eddy punched in the code and placed two wads of money inside the large safe filled with money and guns.

Eddy didn't keep drugs there, only guns and money. Liz respected his privacy. If she needed something, she would ask before she even thought of stealing. Eddy left his aunty five hundred dollars on the table, then he left the crib.

***

Cascade, Atlanta

Buzz was at the Cascade skating rink, posted at a table, as he waited for Ed and Jason. Things had been going smoothly for him, especially with Ashanti and her crew on the team.

Buzz wanted to keep Ashanti a big secret because he didn't want the drama to lead back to him. If the mess did, he would let Eddy handle it. He taught his young boy well.

With a whole list of dudes he wanted Ashanti to set up, he knew he would have to send some reinforcement, just in case shit got real. He knew Ashanti and her girls could handle themselves. If not, things could get very deadly for them.

Buzz wanted Eddy to arrive first, so he could put a bug in his ear. Checking his Cartier watch, he saw Eddy walk in, as if on cue.

"What up, shawty?" Eddy embraced Buzz, taking off his Gucci shades. "Glad you here. I want to tell you this before Jason come," Buzz said.

"What happened?"

"I need you to keep a close eye on Ashanti. She about to go at some heavy hitters and ops, and I need you to make sure her and her girls don't get hurt, please," Buzz requested.

"You want me to babysit?"

"No, just keep an eye on her."

Coke Girlz

"Ok, I'ma do it for you, but I think you should tell Jason."
"Fuck no. I'm still their uncle. I am looking like a snake."
"What if he finds out anyway?" Ed asked as Jason walked inside the place.
"Talk sports," Buzz said as Jason approached.
"So, you think you got all the sense?" Jason said, sitting down.
"Huh?" Buzz played dumb.
"Nigga, you got Ashanti on dumb missions," Jason said, seeing Buzz's eyebrows raise.
"Jason, she is our only way of taking over and getting rid of the ops on both sides," Buzz said.
"I agree. Let's get this money," Jason said as Buzz smiled, glad his nephew was on board.

Romell Tukes

Coke Girlz

Chapter 18

Zone 6, Atlanta

Faith was home, getting ready for her date with the handsome young man from Applebee's. They'd been talking for a few days and she finally agreed to let him take her on a date. What he didn't know was it would be a double date.

She wore a black Gucci top and bottom set, with heels.

"Gurl, you look good," Faith said, looking at herself in the mirror. She was waiting on Elisa to come pick her up so she could pull up on Dugg with a surprise.

Faith knew Dugg was getting money because her home-girl knew he worked for a nigga, Woop, out of Zone 4.

She called Elisa to see where she was at because her grandmom was sleep and she didn't want to wake her up.

"Where you at, bitch?" Faith asked, leaving her room and closing her door softly.

"Outside. Hurry up," Elisa said, with the music up loud.

"Turn that music down before you wake up my grandmom," Faith whispered into the phone.

"Bitch, come on," Elisa said, hurrying up.

Faith's dad was in and out of jail for violating his federal parole. He was a serious bank robber. Growing up with him in and out her life, a father figure was never there for Faith. Her mother died giving birth to her. She'd heard good things about her mom, how she was a good Christian woman, who had a thing for bad boys.

Growing up with her grandmom present, she was raised under the old school law. Her grandmom didn't play. She was strict.

Since she was a kid, Faith had dreams of becoming rich and famous. She had a quick temper and was known for having a quick fuse and beating a bitch's ass. Walking outside, she texted Dugg, telling him she had a surprise for him and needed his location.

"Damn, about time." Elisa looked at Faith when she got in the car.

"Bitch, I had to look cute."

Elisa laughed as she drove off in her new car she'd brought with the money she had left from Ashanti.

"I see. So, what's this about, since you ain't tell me shit on the phone?" Elisa asked, turning down the music.

"It's a dude, named Dugg, I bagged. I hear he moving a lot of weed, pills, and he sell a little coke," Faith said.

"Does Ashanti know about this?"

"Yeah, I texted her," Faith replied.

"So, what's the plan?" Elisa was a little pumped up.

"I don't know. I wanted to surprise him and act like we're girlfriends," Faith said.

"What?" Elisa stopped at a red light.

"Come on, Elisa. We gotta make this shit seem real." Faith saw that Dugg had texted his location, which was his crib, oddly.

"We cousins, and I don't like girls. But I will play your little game. You just better not fucking touch me. I'm dead ass serious." Elisa was upset.

"Ok. Chill out."

"You got the gun?" Elisa asked.

"Yeah." Faith pulled out a glock 30 handgun.

"You know how to use it?" Elisa joked but was serious.

"Yes, I'm from Zone 6, bitch," Faith bragged. Zone 6 was known for violence.

"Where we going?"

"West End. Go to Smith Street, building 71, apartment ten."

"Damn, he thirsty," Elisa said.

"Facts, but I'm going to give him all the juice he needs," Elisa laughed.

***

Zone 4, Atlanta

Dugg had just got out of the shower. He had a towel wrapped around his small, chiseled waist. He was in a rush to put some cologne on,

Coke Girlz

so he could smell good for his company. He couldn't help but wonder what she had in store for him.

When he saw her, he couldn't help but stare at her beauty. So, when he received her info, he didn't hesitate to call.

Dugg sold weight all over Zone 4, only weed and pills. He played with coke when the weed and pill game slowed up. He worked for his cousin, Woop, from Oakland City.

He rushed to get dressed, and as soon as he got fully dressed, the doorbell rang. When the door opened, he saw two bad bitches that were breathtaking.

"Hey. Surprise," Faith said smiling.

"Damn, it's two of you?" Dugg was caught off guard.

"This is my girl, Lisa," Faith said.

"Hey, sexy," Elisa said, acting as if she was Liea.

"Come inside wit all dat sexiness out there." Dugg sucked his teeth, looking at their ass and body. He couldn't wait to fuck both of them.

"This is nice," Faith said, walking into the living room and placing her purse on the table.

"So y'all want to go out? It's only 11pm," Dugg said, sitting between them, looking at their thighs and cute feet.

"Nah. How about we get nasty," Elisa said.

"Ok. I'm down." Dugg started taking off his clothes. He pulled out his big cock and stood in front of Faith's face so she could suck it. Faith knew he was too big, so she wasn't about to try to suck that big cock.

Faith pulled the gun out of her purse as Elisa rubbed Dugg's balls, and he closed his eyes.

"Open up," Faith said, pointing a gun at his penis.

Dugg opened his eyes, wondering if a vibrator was against his dick.

"What the fuck?" He opened his eyes to see a gun on his cock.

"Elisa, check the room for drugs and money." Faith got up and lifted her gun to his head.

"Calm down, shawty. Money is in the mattress, if that's all y'all want." Dugg was still horny, and Faith shook her head.

Elisa went for his mattress. She found a lot of money and ecstasy pills under it.

"Gurl, this nigga up," Elisa yelled, bagging everything in a Louis Vuitton pillowcase.

"We up, so hurry up," Faith yelled back, seeing Dugg looking for something towards the couch.

"Can I still get that threesome?" Dugg asked before she slapped him with the gun.

"Look under the couch. I believe there is something under there," Faith said.

Elisa lifted the cushions and saw money and guns. She got a garbage bag out of the kitchen and filled the bag up. Faith looked at Dugg before shooting him twice in the heart. She flinched pulling the trigger, but she liked it. They left $125,000 richer.

Chapter 19

College Park, Georgia

Ashanti, Elisa, and Faith met up the next night in a park near Ashanti's mom's crib. Since Ashanti moved out of her mom's crib, their relationship had been off and distant, but Ashanti knew, sooner or later, they would make up.

Right now, her main focus was trying to get to a bag. Since she'd been killing and robbing, she started to feel like her heart was turning colder than a winter snowstorm.

She got out of her car to see her cousins awaiting her with big smiles and a brown store bag.

"What's going on with y'all?" Ashanti asked, looking at them both.

"We did it, bitch," Faith said, handing Ashanti the bag of money with her cut from the lick.

"Damn, how much is this?" Ashanti looked in the brown bag.

"$42,000 a piece, that nigga was holding," Elisa said.

"Did anybody see y'all? Did y'all leave anything that could trace back to us?" Ashanti had to ask because she didn't want to get jammed up.

Ashanti had been watching a lot of forensic TV shows on how to get away with murders and crimes. Watching crime shows was her little guilty pleasure.

"We should be good. It was too easy," Elisa said, wanting to do it again, like a kid riding the rollercoaster for the first time.

"Ok. Well, you both need to lay low for a while. I got something in the making I think is gonna be very beneficial. I gotta go meet Sammy now," Ashanti said, tucking the money in her Chanel purse.

"Faith trying to go to Miami for her birthday in a few weeks," Elisa said.

"Set it up. We gonna need a vacation soon, trust and believe," Ashanti added.

"Do you think this shit gonna get back to us?" Faith asked.

"I hope not," Ashanti said.

"Dese niggas be having so much beef. Bitch, they won't know who did it," Elisa said.

"Facts. And who would assume three bad bitches is behind this?" Ashanti told her girls, making a point.

"I guess y'all right," Faith said.

"We good. We just gotta keep finding the money-getting niggas," Elisa said.

"I'm starting to think you like this shit a lot more than Ashanti" Faith joked but was serious.

"It's easy money. It's like taking candy from a handicap kid." Elisa made them laugh.

"I have to go. I'll call y'all broke bitches when I'm ready to ride on this new nigga," Ashanti said, leaving.

"Ok," they both said.

***

Riverdale, Georgia

Ashanti was on her way to meet one of her best friends, Sammy, at her second job. Ashanti and Sammy had been cool since they were kids. Some people thought they were sisters, considering how much they looked alike.

Sammy worked at a strip club three days a week. The other three days, she worked overnight at a Sam's Club. Sammy had just had a newborn, so she was working hard to provide because her baby's father was a deadbeat.

Pulling into the parking lot, she saw a call from her Uncle Buzz, but she didn't answer. Ashanti already knew what he wanted. In an hour, he wanted to meet her.

Ashanti didn't like talking on the phone about crimes or missions anymore, after she watched a true crime story on how two dudes got locked up from wiretaps talking about three murders they'd done.

Coke Girlz

She texted Sammy, who should have been on her break. After finding a parking spot in the front row, she saw Sammy come out, looking a straight mess, with her hair and nails undone.

Ashanti climbed out of the Benz. She saw a text from Alex, but she left him on read.

"Hey." Ashanti gave her girl a hug.

"I been stressed. Sav got arrested a few days ago with a gun and some drugs, but he took the hit for some nigga he was working for in Zone 4." Sammy took a deep breath.

"Ain't no way."

"Yeah, gurl, and the nigga he took the weight for is a big-time dealer and won't even bail him out."

"That's foul. How old is Sav?" Ashanti knew her little brother was younger than her.

"Seventeen. I been trying to get him bail, but you know I had the baby, so I called you for help. I need like ten grand and I'll pay you back," Sammy said with begging eyes.

Ashanti went into the car and counted $15,000 out of the money Elisa had just given her.

"Here you go, and you don't owe me shit. This is what friends are for," Ashanti said.

Sammy almost cried because her little brother was her world, and her everything.

"Thank you so much."

"That's nothing. But who was Sav working for?" Ashanti said, as a lightbulb went off in her head.

"Some nigga named Woop," Sammy told her, checking the time because she had to get back to work.

"Oh, he shady." Ashanti took a mental note of the name in her mind. "Woop."

"Hell yeah, but I'ma get back to work before them crackers start tripping. Thank you again," Sammy said, giving her another hug before walking back into the store.

Ashanti was thinking about putting Sammy down with the crew, but she knew her cousins didn't know her, and they would act funny. Ashanti also knew Sammy was not that type of girl.

83

Romell Tukes

She drove to meet her annoying uncle.

Coke Girlz

Chapter 20

Downtown, Atlanta

Uncle Buzz waited for his niece with Ed in his truck, parked at a twenty-four gas station.

"I can handle this dude. You don't need Ashanti to do it," Ed said, texting his friend on his iPhone.

"Now why would I do that?" Uncle Buzz let out a chuckle.

"That's your niece, and she may not be ready for him. Dude not a dummy. He may peep her game and bust a move." Ed made a point.

"Listen, she signed up for the game, so she gotta deal with whatever comes with it," Buzz said.

Ed shook his head. He was starting to see a side of Buzz that made him second guess who he truly was as a man.

"I'ma still look out," Ed said.

"That's what she got her crew for. I need you to pull up on that nigga Fry from Zone 1. He been owing me for a few months now," Buzz stated, pouring himself a cup of dark liquor.

"Damn, you let him slide that long, shawty? I heard that fool sniffing dog food," Ed said. That was the street rumor.

"He what?" Buzz shouted.

"Nigga, he getting high wit your shit, cuz," Ed repeated, seeing Ashanti's car pull into the lot.

"I want you to go get that nigga tonight. I got two bricks for you," Buzz said.

"Nah, I'll do that for free. Fry did some bullshit awhile back to my little cousin," Ed said.

"Ight, let me go holla at this little bitch." Buzz climbed out of the truck and met Ashanti halfway.

Ed noticed how fly she was looking and almost bit his tongue. He liked her swag. He could tell she was a real gangster bitch with class.

He locked eyes with her as she talked with Buzz, and she waved at him.

***

"I need you and your girls to do whatever it is y'all do but be smart. I don't need anything coming back to me, Ashanti," Uncle Buzz told her.

"I know how to move." She sucked her teeth.

"I hope so."

"Who is the nigga? Where he from? Give me the 411 so I can get on it. And what's in it for you?" Ashanti asked the main question he was waiting for.

"His name is Woop, from Zone 4. He is doing big things under one of my rivals," Buzz stated.

Ashanti remember the name from talking to Sammy less than an hour ago, so she was more than willing to go on this mission.

"I'll get on it this week," Ashanti said as she saw Ed stare at her sexually.

"I'll text you his location when I get it confirmed."

"Will do," she said, turning to leave, giving Ed a good look at her nice, perfect ass.

***

Zone 1, Atlanta

Elisa and Ashanti drove through the worst section in Zone 1, called Da Bluff, which was the dope capital of the city of Atlanta.

They were going to buy Elisa a used car and some guns from a nigga called Goode. He sold cars and guns.

"How do you want to do this shit with Woop? I think he used to fuck with a girl I know," Elisa said.

"I been watching Set It Off and I-"

"Hold on, bitch, you watching Set It Off? We ain't robbing banks," Elisa said, as she cut her off.

"They had good tactics. We can use some on these niggas out here," Ashanti said seriously.

Coke Girlz

"Bitch, you bugging," Elisa said.

They pulled up to a trap house. There was a dude with big glasses standing in front of the house, looking nervous.

"I think we should just kick the door in on some Rambo shit," Ashanti said.

"I ain't fucking with you. Is this our guy?" Elisa said, seeing an ugly dude with a book bag and car keys.

"Y'all Moe people?" Goode said, leaning into the Benz window.

"Yes," Elisa stated.

"Here, just give me twenty bands," Goode said, looking around and passing Elisa the car keys and a book bag full of guns.

"Twenty?" Elisa said.

"Yes."

"I thought it was 15,000?" Elisa could tell he was playing games.

"It was, but I'm out here risking my life," Goode said.

"Here, gurl, pay him so he can get out of here," Ashanti said, passing her the rest of the money to go with Elisa's amount.

"Thank you," Goode said, pointing at the used Lexus Sedan that was now Elisa's.

Romell Tukes

Coke Girlz

Chapter 21

Stone Mountain, Georgia

The streets were talking, and they were talking serious. Niggas were putting big money on Jason's head because everybody thought Jason was the one who killed Durk, or had him murdered.

Durk had a lot of love and family in the Stone Mountain area and Clayton County, where he grew up. Jason didn't give a fuck. He rode through the streets with the top down on his Benz, blasting rap music.

Since Durk was out of the picture, he'd been locking down the streets with his crew of GDs that he was tight with. Jason was not in a gang, but he fucked with the gang bangers when it came to money. Jason pulled over near a corner store, to see one of his worker on the block, patching work.

"I see you, Mike, out here grinding, shawty," Jason said.

"Man, it's hot as hell out here, playboy. Them New York niggas that came down here scamming, you know who I'm talking about?" Mike asked.

Jason heard there were four brothers out in his land, scamming, from New York. But he didn't care because they were not selling drugs.

"I know who you talking about," Jason said as a bad chick came out the store, smiling at him.

"They killed two of ours last night," Mike stated.

"How the fuck am I just hearing of this, bruh?" Jason said, pissed.

"Your phone was off," Mike said.

"Man, y'all niggas on some bullshit, fucking up the money. Who they hit up?" Jason couldn't believe he was just now hearing of this shit.

"Tooia and DeeDee."

"Tooia?" Jason had a liking for Tooia. He was the youngest of the camp.

89

"Yeah, but niggas is saying them New York niggas is Durk cousins, or so dumb shit. But I never seen them together or nothing," Mike said, looking at two crackheads call him over from across the street.

Jason was thinking, while a black Impala sneaked down the block and two men hopped out. But Jason was on point, unlike Mike.

Boom.
Boom.
Boom.
Boom.

Jason shot one of the men who had hopped out of the Impala. The other man fired two shots back, hitting Mike.

Bloc.
Bloc.

When Mike's body hit the ground, Jason ducked. Then he popped up, firing two shoots into the man's chest, murking both of them.

Jason killed both of them and ran past two females, jumping in his car and peeling off, getting away.

His heart was racing. He couldn't believe he just hit two niggas. He knew it was time to get low for a while.

***

Zone 4, Atlanta

Woop and his boy, Fresh, drove to his crib on the West End with two bad bitches they'd met at a club downtown.

Woop let his boy whip his new candy red g-wagon Benz truck through the hood he was in control of.

This was Woop's hood, the West End, where he was born and raised. He sold weight all throughout Zone 4. His plug, Mills, was his first cousin, supplying him with the purest work he ever had.

Hustling and partying was Woop's life. He was twenty-two years old and doing big things in the city. When one of his workers,

Coke Girlz

Dugg, got killed, he was fucked up. But he knew it was a part of the game.

Woop had a feeling it was some Crip niggas from Campbellton Road they were beefing with over a bitch.

"You think they good?" Fresh said, looking in the rearview at the chicks in the backseat.

"They straight, bro. We just fuck them, pass them, and kick them out," Woop said in a low pitch voice as he smiled.

"Ight."

Woop put on a smile for the women, showing his diamond grill.

Fresh parked in front of the two-story house Woop used to stash drugs and money, and fuck bitches.

"Let's go, ladies." Woop got out and walked in the crib with Fresh by his side, checking his pockets for condoms. This was an every night event for them.

Once in the house, the door closed, and they heard a click.

"What the fuck?" Fresh said, turning around towards the chicks.

When Fresh and Woop saw what was going on, they knew it was a set-up.

"Get on y'all knees," Ashanti said to them both.

"Fuck." Woop did as they asked.

"Bitch, you got me fucked up," Fresh yelled.

"Bruh, chill, it's cool," Woop said.

"Nah, fuck these hoes." Fresh was drunk.

"Tell your man to chill," Elisa told Woop.

"Bitch, you know who I am?" Fresh puffed up at Elisa about to hit her.

Bloc.

Bloc.

Bloc.

"Oh shit," Woop said, seeing her hit Fresh in the chest, dropping him.

"Everything in the grill in my back yard." Woop already knew what it was.

"Thank you," Ashanti said before she blew his brains out.

91

They ran out back and found two suitcases full of drugs and money.

Coke Girlz

Chapter 22

Zone 4, Atlanta

Outside the two story house, Faith was patiently waiting. She'd followed her girls from the lounge, where Ashanti and Elisa bagged Woop and Fresh.
She was tailing Woop in the g-wagon truck the whole time. She saw this on TV a few times and kept it in the back of her mind.
Elisa and Ashanti rushed out from the side of the house, in heels, with a gun and suitcase in both of their hands.
"Dese bitches crazy, crazy," she said out loud, starting up Elisa's new car.
"Drive, bitch," Elisa yelled, jumping in the car, sweating like she just did an hour of burpees.
"Ok." Faith pulled off.
Ashanti opened the suitcase and saw she had keys of tan bricks inside.
"Open yours," Ashanti told Elisa, who was already on it.
Elisa saw stacks of blue faces neatly stacked inside the suitcase, filling it up.
"Wow, we about to be lit, lit, bitch," Faith said from the driver's seat.
"Pull over at this gas station," Ashanti said, pointing at the gas station across the street.
"Bitch, you tripping. We just killed two niggas back there," Elisa stated.
"I gotta piss," Ashanti said, moving around and holding her crotch, like she had a penis.
"Ight, damn," Faith said, pulling over so she could piss.
Ashanti rushed into the public dirty restroom that smelled like piss and shit.
"Ewwwwwww," she said, seeing doodoo in one of the toilets.
She went into the next stall, which was a little cleaner, and pissed. Her piss came out hard. She'd been holding it since she left the club.

93

When she wiped herself, flushed the toilet, and went to wash her hands, the sink water was off.

"Bitch," she yelled, looking around. Once she realized it was over for washing her hands, she opened the door and ran into Eddy.

"Oh my god, what the fuck? You scared the shit outta me," she said, holding her chest.

"You good?" Ed asked.

"Yes. Why are you here?" She found it weird he was there.

"I been following you since you went to the club, to be honest," he said.

"Why?"

"To make sure you were good. I know Woop gets down," Eddy said, as two chicks crept around the corner with guns.

"Ashanti, you good?" Faith said, looking at Ed up and down, thinking he was an op, or Woop's people.

"Yes," Ashanti replied.

"Ok. He's cute," Elisa said, leaving them alone.

"I have to go, but thank you for checking on me," Ashanti said, walking off, smelling his strong men's cologne.

"Sure." He threw up the deuces.

"Ashanti, who was that sexy ass nigga?" Faith said.

"My peoples," Ashanti replied.

"Put me on with your people then" Elisa said

"Hell nah. If anything, he all me," Ashanti said, looking out the window as the car peeled off. She watched Ed as he got in the car behind them.

"What we gonna do with all this money and drugs?" Faith asked.

"We keeping all the money, and taking half of the drugs. I have to give some to my fat ass uncle," Ashanti said as they drove back to her crib.

"I'm cool with that," Elisa said.

"Me too," Faith said, driving.

"We going to Miami in a few days," Ashanti stated.

"Ok," Elisa smiled.

"I can't wait," Faith said, listening to Hot 107.9.

Coke Girlz

"Me either," Ashanti said, nodding her head to the beat.

Romell Tukes

Coke Girlz

Chapter 23

USP Atlanta Federal Prison

Megan arrived at work at her usual time, but she was really tired, for some reason. The weather was bad outside. The pouring rain always made her feel drowsy and lazy.

Since Ashanti moved on, she'd been at home, bored and lonely. She'd been going on a few dates, but the males she was coming across weren't worth a second date. The good men were dead or in jail.

Every day she worried about her beautiful daughters, Ashanti and Candra. She knew she raised her children the best way she could, even Jason. Everybody made mistakes in life, so she understood that.

Megan just wanted the best for all her children, so she was stern on being a good parent, a strict parent, and a good role model. When she facetimed Candra every night, she felt so proud of her, unlike how she felt about Ashanti, whom she knew was living a bad life.

A few weeks ago, Megan got word from her cousin, who told her she saw Ashanti chilling with her Uncle Buzz.

When Megan heard this, she knew Ashanti was in something she shouldn't be in. Buzz was a bad person, and Megan did not even want him around her or her kids.

Megan really wanted to cuss Buzz out, and give him a piece of her mind, but she knew he wasn't worth it. Buzz did the same thing with her son, Jason, trying to corrupt him.

"Good morning, Megan," one of her male co-workers said, walking past her on her way to work on a unit she was assigned to.

"Morning, Tim," she replied, seeing the man do a quick glimpse at her pussy print in her tight pants.

Megan wore tight clothes that showed her figure because she knew the inmates needed some eye candy. They had nothing else to look at. She always smelled good, and had her hair and nails done up.

There were a few inmates in the prison she would love to fuck, especially this one young man from New York they called Mell. He would train a few inmates on the unit and was very soft spoken and respectful.

Megan loved dark-skin, tall, handsome muscular men, with tatts and dreads. Every time she would see him, her pussy would be drenched.

Today she was working in Mell's unit and she had to stay focused. She was a strong black woman. A lot of women would look down on prisoners. But if they only knew, some of them were the best of people.

Megan walked in the loud unit with her work bag and saw prisoners watching TV, ironing clothes, playing poker and some staring at her.

When she worked a unit, she was not the super cop type. She was laid back. The correctional officer left from the office, finishing his shift. Megan straighten up the office and wiped down everything with alcohol pads.

On her walkie-talkie, she heard the Rec call, where prisoners could go to work out, outside or in the gym.

"Rec, gentlemen," she yelled into the unit, seeing almost the whole unit get ready to leave.

Megan closed the office door and made her way to the front door to open it, as almost everybody looked at her ass jiggle.

Everybody was rushing outside. It took close to ten minutes to clear out the unit. She was happy the unit was quiet, but there were still a few prisoners left.

Megan checked her watch that said eight am, and walked around the unit to do her rounds, walking around the bottom and top tier to make sure nobody was dead.

Walking from cell to cell, she peeped her head into each cell on a drive by. When she got to a cell on the end in a blind spot, she saw Mell getting dressed in his brief boxers. When she saw his large bulge, her mouth dropped. Mell locked eyes with her, and she was caught. He told her to come in.

Coke Girlz

Megan didn't know what to do, so she paused until he opened the door. She stepped in, and what he did next made her weak in her knees. He dropped his boxers.

"Get undressed, ma. We don't have long," Mell said, as she did as he told her. When he saw her clean shaved phat pussy, he ate her out on his desk, making her go crazy.

Mell bent her over and started to fuck her doggy-style, as his huge cock opened her up.

"Oh my God, Mell," she yelled feeling him in her guts, as he went deeper, making her climax.

Mell did his thing for ten minutes, then kissed her lips before kicking her out of his cell. Megan got herself and hair together. She couldn't even walk straight, the dick was so good. She planned to pay him a visit on the next rec move.

Romell Tukes

Chapter 24

Clark University, Atlanta

"How long we been studying for, bitch? I'm about to fall asleep in this book," said Candra's best friend Aliana.

"We only been here for two hours and it's like you ain't get nothing down pack yet," Candra said, getting frustrated at her friend and sucking her teeth.

"I don't know shit about all this civil law bullshit. Now criminal law, and all the penal codes, I got down packed easy," Alina told her.

They sat in the school study hall, which was open twenty-four hours a day for students to study whenever needed.

"Well you better figure it out," Candra told her, closing her text book, packing up her belongings, and preparing to leave.

"What a friend?" Aliana shook her head with a laugh.

Aliana was a cute white girl with a little butt and big titties. The black dudes in the school loved her, but she had a boyfriend outside of the school she loved to death.

Aliana and Candra stuck together like they were so close and they both had similar ways.

Candra walked back to the dorm, while Aliana went back to studying. She had a big test this week, the finals for the end of the semester.

While walking, Candra got a facetime call from Jason. She saw a bench on her left. She answered the call and took a seat because her hands were filled with books.

"Brother," she said, looking at him on her phone. She could tell he was in a car.

"What up Candra? I ain't heard from your stinking ass in a few days. You ok?" Jason stated.

"Boy, stop. Ain't nothing stinky about this," she spat back, happy to see her brother.

"Whatever, shawty. How's school?"

"Good, hanging in there, doing what I do best," Candra stated.

"I'm proud of you." Jason always knew his sister would be something, ever since they were kids.

"Thanks. But what's going on with Ashanti?" Candra asked, not hearing from Ashanti in a while.

"I don't know, but I don't think she dancing no more." Jason knew Candra already knew her sister was stripping.

"Oh, that's great. I hope she working somewhere better."

"I have no clue," Jason lied, with a funny face. She could tell he meant something more than what he was saying.

"How you been?"

"Same shit, you feel me?"

"Guess so. I spoke to mommy today and she seemed happy, like she hit the lotto," Candra joked.

"Maybe she did. Her tight ass ain't finna tell us if she did," Jason joked on his mom, knowing how selfish she was.

"I gotta go. My boyfriend calling me," Candra said.

"Boyfriend?"

"Yes, I have a boyfriend," she said proudly.

"From where? Who is he? Why you just telling me?" He started to ask all types of questions.

"Because it's none of your business," she spat back.

"Oh, it's like that?"

"Facts. Bye, Jason. Love you," she said, hanging up the facetime call.

Candra smiled and called her new boyfriend back, who had her on high horse.

***

South Beach, Miami

The girls had just landed in Miami a few hours ago. They got settled into their hotel rooms to enjoy their three days out there.

Ashanti, Faith, and Elisa needed to get low after the last robbery.

"I love it out here," Elisa said, drinking a fruity liquor blend.

Coke Girlz

"Gurl, this is your first time out here?" Faith said.

"So. I'm pretty sure there will be more to come," Elisa shot back, fixing her sundress.

The sun was going down, leaving a colorful orange and purple sunset. The view was so nice, people were taking pics outside.

They were at an outside bar, called Tequila, enjoying the evening.

"Fuck all dat, what we doing tonight?" Ashanti asked in her bikini, getting a lot of attention.

"Club G Five?" Faith said.

"I think you gay," Elisa said, making everybody laugh.

"Bitch, please. If I was, you would know because I would stay with a bad bitch," Faith added.

The girls enjoyed their drinks and went back to the hotel to get dressed to go out clubbing.

***

North Miami, Miami

Club The Lexx was off the chain. Everybody came out to 125th in North Miami for the big bash.

The girls had a table in the corner, watching the crazy show down, while the DJ spun the newest Miami artists, and a few Atlanta artists, like Lil Baby and Future's new hits.

"These clubs ain't fucking with ours. We got the best," Ashanti said, waiting on more bottles to arrive. They'd shared two bottles of expensive Moet already, but they wanted to stunt, so they ordered five this go around.

"Atlanta is popping. We really like the new black Mecca," Faith said, tipsy, watching a few dudes eye her. But she was on her period, so she was feisty.

"I gotta pee," Ashanti said, getting up and pulling down her Gucci mini dress that was raising on her thick thighs.

"Hold on, here go the bottle girl. Ain't you paying?" Elisa asked, as two Spanish women with fake asses and titties placed the bottles on the table, fresh out the ice bucket, dripping cold water.

"Y'all got it. Treat," Ashanti said, walking off. She still had her cup in her hand, making her way through the crowd.

Ashanti felt someone touch her ass, but she looked and saw nobody's hand near.

On her way to the bathroom, she saw a young, handsome brother with a lot of jewelry on and a nice Givenchy outfit. He was looking good.

She was rocking with Alex because she was trying to level up and elevate. But Alex wanted to leech off her, and she didn't respect that.

The handsome man-made eye contact with her, and she liked his light brown eyes off the rip.

"What up, shawty?" the man said, with an Atlanta accent.

"Shawty?" she asked, knowing he wasn't from Miami.

"Yeah, or I can call you beautiful," he said loudly, over the club music.

"Beautiful sounds better," she flirted back.

"I'm Heat."

"I'm Ashanti." She shook his hand.

"That's you and your girls over there?" Heat asked.

"Yeah, we from Atlanta."

"I can tell," Heat said.

"Oh yeah. Where you from, because you sound like you from Atlanta?"

"I am. I been living in Miami for a while now," Heat said, letting people pass them to use the bathrooms.

"Ok. What do you do for a living, because I see you doing it big?" She looked at the ice around his neck and wrist.

"I am a businessman," he told her, but she read between the lines.

"Oh, I catch you drift."

"I don't think you do because I really own a business, and I do real estate," Heat told her as he saw dollar signs in her eyes.

Coke Girlz

"That's good, but I have to use the bathroom and get back to my girls. Have a good night," she said, about to walk off.

"Wait," Heat shouted.

"Take my card and call me. I would like to see you before you go back to the A," he said, handing her a business card.

"Ok, sure." She took the card, smiling and walking off, as he looked at her phat ass clap in her dress.

***

Riverdale, Georgia

Mills had a big mini mansion he shared with his beautiful black queen Franchesca.

Tonight, was their ten year anniversary, so Franchesca had their bedroom lit up with candles.

They were all over each other, like two wild monkeys.

"I got a surprise for you, my King," she said, going low on him.

Franchesca was a pretty brown, thick, short haired woman, with phat lips.

She saw his swollen cock and slowly sucked and licked the tip, loving dick in her mouth. She was sucking and slurping on his erect penis.

"Mmmm," Mills' moaned as his girl took his mind off the streets. Things had been crazy lately. The more she went deep, the more it was a hefty mouthful.

Franchesca loved sucking dick because she would always achieve her own explosive orgasm. She went deep, bobbing her head up and down, until he nutted in her mouth.

Mills was ready to fuck, as he turned her to the side and entered her tightness. He was soon fucking her with long deliberate thrusts, pulling her into his dick.

Her pussy was clinging tightly around his thick cock, as he fucked her, while lifting her leg in the air and making her catch a powerful orgasm.

"Oh my, that's it," she screamed, squirting everywhere. They spent the night fucking in crazy positions, making up shit.

Chapter 25

Zone 1, Atlanta

Faith had just gotten back from her trip to Miami with her cousins yesterday. She'd had a ball on the beaches, shopping, and hitting up the hottest clubs.

She hadn't gotten any real sleep since she left Atlanta, so today, after running around, she planned to sleep all day. Faith had just bought a new car. At first she wasn't but seeing Ashanti in her Benz and Elisa in her Lexus, she had to follow their lead, so she copped a BMW 4 series.

Being able to push a luxury car made her feel like a boss bitch. She loved the feeling of power and success. The profit of the last lick had her bank account right, and she was on her way to check out a new apartment.

Growing up in Zone 1 was cool, but she felt like it was time to relocate and move around with her new lifestyle. Never in a million years would she have seen herself as a jack-girl.

Robbing niggas made her feel an extra push of empowerment, but she knew it was very dangerous, and Atlanta niggas were about that gunplay.

Her biggest fear was someone finding out who was robbing niggas, but now they had guns. She planned to be ready for any backfires.

Driving through Simpson Road, niggas were everywhere, ice grilling the car. But Faith had a XD40 with 13 shots in her purse, just in case a nigga liked trying her. Faith pulled over at the store to grab some wraps to roll up some good exotic weed she got from her neighbor.

It was hot and muggy outside, so she wore tight shorts, showing her thick thighs. Her top showed her flat tummy, and her open toe Chanel sandals exposed her pedicured feet.

Walking in the store, she caught everybody's attention, but a few dudes knew her from around the way.

Faith almost walked into a short man with long, thick dreads. He was far from handsome but the way he rocked his designer clothes and expensive jewelry, she knew he was somebody.

"Nice ride, shawty," the short man said, standing face to face with her, about to walk past.

"Thanks, handsome," she said, showing her white teeth, making him feel like he was Chris Brown, as she walked to the counter.

"What's your name?" he asked, turning around and looking at her phat ass busting out her jean shorts.

"Faith."

"I'm Kay Money."

"How about I just call you Kay?" she asked, making him feel like a broke nigga.

"I got money, so you gotta add da you dig."

"What's money to you?" She stopped and looked at his lazy eye, wandering down her to her puffy pussy print as she paid for the blunts.

"Millions."

"Oh, so that's you?"

"Let me show you. Take my number and call me later," Kay said.

"I'll think about it," she said, letting him say his number while she logged it in her phone.

Kay watched her strut off and his penis grew hard, even the store clerk saw it and shook her head.

***

Kay Money sold weight for his Uncle Mills. At twenty-two years old, he was up. Mills would bless him with so many keys at once, he would flood the whole Zone 1.

Last year, Kay won a million-dollar lawsuit that he was still sitting on, so he didn't have to sell drugs, but he really wanted the street credit.

He was never a street nigga. His mom raised him in a good household, until she passed, due to cancer, last year.

Coke Girlz

Running the streets with his crew, he felt untouchable. But the only reason he was good in the streets was because of Mills. In Zone 1, Mills was the big dawg. Everybody respected him, and he had a crew of killers on deck.

Kay couldn't wait to get up with Faith. He knew she would be the best fuck of the summer. He'd never seen her on Simpson Road before, so that was good. He also liked how she was pushing a nice car, which meant she had a bag, or a boyfriend.

He didn't care if she had a man, or not. He just wanted to fuck and tell his boys about it.

***

Stone Mountain, Georgia

Jason's girl, India, used his car to drive around, handling business. Her car caught a flat tire last night, so she had to get it checked and fixed sometime today.

Since Jason was out of town, somewhere in Alabama, making money moves, she had time to do her. And she was doing just that. She pulled up to an apartment complex and texted her ex-boyfriend, Chad, who had just come home from jail. She had plans to fuck him in Jason's Benz truck, the same way Jason fucked a lot of bitches in there that she knew about.

Chad came home tatted and real stocky, after a five-year bid. Before he went away, he and India couldn't get enough of each other. When he got locked up, she ran off with Jason, crushing his heart.

She wasn't built to do a bid, but she used to talk a good game, as if she was his ride or die, until shit hit the fan.

India saw Chad come out in a sweat suit, with his dreads hanging. She couldn't wait to get some dick from him, especially if he hit it like he did five years ago, when he used to kill her shit.

"Hey," she said, as he opened the door and got inside.

"You look good. Who truck is this?" Chad asked, kissing her on the cheek.

"Damn, no mouth action?" she asked, staring at him.
"Sorry," he kissed her lips.
"This is my sister's truck," she lied, with a straight face.
"Ok. Where you wanna go?"
"Hotel, or we can fuck in the back. I really wanna suck your dick. You know I miss da monster," she said, looking at his crotch.
"What you waiting on?" Chad was reaching for his cock when the driver door flew open and five masked men with guns snatched India out of the driver's seat.
"Help," she yelled, as the kidnappers tossed her in a commercial van and pulled off into the night.

Coke Girlz

Chapter 26

Cobb County, Georgia

Somewhere in a barn, India was tied up on the floor, crying, as hay and chicken shit stuck to her legs and arms. The barn was empty, besides the few chickens and cows she saw to her left. She knew she was in the country somewhere, but she didn't know where because she was blindfolded the whole ride.

A door slid open. She saw a group of men enter with AK 47 assault rifles with lemon squeeze grips.

"India," an unfamiliar voice said, coming closer to her.

When she saw the man, she looked confused as to what was really going on.

"Who are you, and what's going on?" she said, looking at the older man. When India looked deeper into crowd, she couldn't believe who she saw standing amongst the kidnappers, Chad.

"Don't look too surprised, bitch. You think I was gonna let you suck me off after you left me for dead and crossed me?" Chad asked.

"Are you serious, Chad? That was five years ago," she said.

"To you, but to me, it's still new. So let me explain to you what's going on, because you look lost. Your boyfriend had my boy, Durk, killed, or he killed him. This is Lil Hiss, Durk's uncle, my plug and nig, bruh. So, you finna call your man and let him know we got you, and he gotta give himself up so we can end this, cutie." He handed her an iPhone he'd found in her purse to call Jason.

India's hand was shaking uncontrollably as she dialed his number.

"Put it on speaker, bitch," Lil Hiss said hoping to bring closure to his little nephew's death.

Jason picked up on the fourth ring, and the room got quiet.

"Hello," Jason answered.

"Baby, I was kidnapped. I need your help," she cried into the phone, with real tears.

Jason started clapping into the phone, making everybody look around.

"Bitch, you good. Let me guess, Chad got you," Jason said. Everybody heard it.

"Huh, how did you know?" she asked, thinking this was all a game or something.

"I didn't go outta town. I tricked you into believing I did so I could see how shady you was. I slashed your tires, too, just so you could use my SUV, so niggas could get at you." Jason shocked everybody there.

"But why?" she yelled.

"You fucked two of my mans, bitch. You think I ain't know? We got a code, bros before hoes. I knew you was waiting on me to go O.T. so you can meet up with Chad, so I lied. I watched them kidnap your dumb ass," he said.

Lil Hiss took the phone. "Nigga, fuck all the games. When I see you, I'ma kill your bitch ass," Lil Hiss yelled into the phone before blowing her head off.

***

Zone 4, Atlanta

Style and his best friend, Top Shot, drove through the Oakland City section, blasting music in Top Shot's Cutlass, about to rob a local drug dealer named Apple, who worked for a plug named Coral.

This was Style's life, robbing and selling to make ends meet. He lived with a little chick named DeeDee, from the West End section.

Style was making a name for himself in the city, but he was also making a lot of enemies. Whatever he got from the licks he went on, he would bust it down with Top Shot.

The drugs they would bust down with their young boys in the West End and College Park area.

"This the building," Top Shot said, pulling over in front of Apple's stash house that he'd been hearing about.

Coke Girlz

Top Shot was a Haitian kid, dark, with five big dreads that were dirty and nasty, looking as if he didn't take care of them.

"Let's go," Style said, already pulling out his AR 22 assault rifle that held over a hundred rounds in the drum.

"Nah, bruh, hold on. Let me peep it out first. I don't trust that bitch, RiRi. She used to fuck with dude," Top Shot said.

"Ight, hurry up," Style said, watching him get out, look up and down the block, and cross the street.

In the blink of an eye, two gunmen snuck out from behind the building with guns, dressed in all black.

Top Shot was so focused on the lick that he ain't even peep the play. Style got out the car and yelled to his best friend. But by the time he turned around, it was too late.

Bloc. Bloc. Bloc. Bloc. Bloc. Bloc. Bloc.

Top Shot's body was rattled with bullets. Style fired nonstop at the men, until he killed both of them with the AR 22.

Style went to see if Top Shot had a chance, but he had no pulse, making him shed a tear. He got off his knees, climbing in the cutlass, and racing off, thinking about his friend's murder, and who was the cause of it.

Coke Girlz

Chapter 27

Downtown, Atlanta

Kay was talking over the slow jams playing in the brand-new Porsche, as he drove Faith to their first date, which he begged her for. At first, Faith played hard to get, but she eventually gave in and let him take her out to eat and to the Trap Museum, which they were headed to now, on the famous Peach Tree Street.

Faith wasn't even listening to him talk. She was listening to the music on V-103, playing back-to-back 702, an old school RnB group.

This was the worst date she'd ever been on in her life. Faith had never met a person who could talk about themselves for hours, nonstop. To make shit worse, his breath had been smelling like shit all night. She cursed herself, but she had a bigger vision.

"You straight, shawty? You been quiet all night," Kay asked, pulling into the famous Trap Museum he'd been to many times.

"I'm just listening, handsome," she replied.

"Ok, good, but I was saying I been stacking millions since a young nigga out cha," Kay bragged, getting out the car, and not even opening the door for her.

"How old are you again?" Faith said, climbing out in a nice pair of red bottom heels and a tight little jean dress made by Dior.

"Age ain't nothing but a number," he shot back, walking inside with his chains dangling, feeling like he was the man.

"Goofy," Faith said, watching Kay run up to people, shaking their hands. She played the wall, texting Ashanti and Elisa her location in a group text. A few handsome brothers eyed her, but she was focused on her job.

"Why you standing there? Let's walk around. They just put some new T.I. shit in the back," Kay said, grabbing her hand.

"How about we just go back to your place and fuck?" she stated flat out, seeing she had finally caught his attention.

"Let's roll. You should have been said something," Kay stated.

"Where you live anyway?" she asked so she could text it to her crew. But they were already parked outside.

"Ben Hill. I got a little two-story spot I use for shit."

"I'ma use the little girl room."

"Hurry up, sexy," he said, looking at her ass when she walked off, feeling his erection harden.

Faith texted her girls his crib location, but she had the location enabled on her phone anyway, so they could follow and keep tabs. Faith had a feeling Kay was finna be a big move for them.

***

"There she go now, coming out the front with that ugly dude," Elisa said, sitting in the rental car, watching Faith and Kay.

"He icy, though," Ashanti said.

"That's about it. He built like a little kid," Elisa joked.

"He look like that retarded brother you don't wanna take out in public," Ashanti added, laughing.

"Bitch, you dead wrong for that," Elisa said, seeing the Porsche with Faith inside pull off.

"What you been doing with your money?" Ashanti asked.

"Saving it, but I been thinking we should all move in together," Elisa replied.

"Hell nah. That will make it easy for our enemy to get us," Ashanti said, as if she'd already thought about it.

"We don't have enemies because nobody knows what we doing," Elisa told her.

"For now." Ashanti saw a text pop up on her phone from her brother, telling her to call.

"This nigga smart enough to move to Ben Hill, I see," Elisa said, entering a middle-class neighborhood, full of houses.

"We finna see." Ashanti pulled out a FN and a P90 small rifle, ready for whatever came their way. Ashanti was practicing all night how to use all the weapons she had, so when it was time to bust, she wouldn't fuck up.

Coke Girlz

***

Ben Hill, Atlanta

Kay got out and opened the door for her, in a rush. Faith laughed at how corny and goofy Kay was.

"I see you a gentleman now."

"I can be at times," he shot back, unlocking his front door and entering his home he barely came to. The place was junky, with a bad odor. She turned her nose up to the disgusting place.

"Make yourself at home. I'll go grab some condoms. I want you naked by the time I come back," Kay said, slapping her big ass.

Faith felt violated. She rushed to open the door, waving for Ashanti and Elisa to come in. And they did just that, in a matter of seconds.

"Ok, good." Ashanti handed Elisa a gun.

Seconds later, Kay walked out ass naked, with a four-inch penis sticking up, erect.

All three of them laughed as they aimed weapons at him. Kay froze with a bottle of liquor in his hand.

"Where is all the money at, fuck nigga? And you better be holding, since you came up short in that department." Faith pointed the Glock 40 at his penis.

"I have everything in a shoe box under the couch and in my mattress in the back," Kay said, giving up his re-up.

Without any talk, Ashanti and Faith went on the hunt for the money, while Elisa waited.

Moments later, Ashanti and Faith came back with close to $20,000 a piece in their hand.

"What the fuck is this?" Ashanti was mad.

"That's all I have, besides the jewelry. My car is leased, clothes be fake. I'm not even up to a key of coke yet," Kay told the truth. He'd been lying the whole time he was telling Faith he had millions and was the plug to get in her panties.

Boc. Boc. Boc. Boc. Boc. Boc. Boc.

Faith continued to fire into his head, until the glock jammed. She was so mad that he played her. They all left, pissed. The ride to Ashanti's crib was quiet.

Coke Girlz

Chapter 28

Zone 3, Atlanta

Eddy drove through Mechanicsville projects, looking for Tecca, his cousin, who had the projects on a chokehold with the coke Tecca was getting from Eddy.

Selling drugs was something Eddy always disliked because he saw what it could do to black families in urban communities.

Robbing and killing the bad guys was more so his speed. Ever since he was a little kid, he wanted to be some type of ghetto hero.

Buzz had been calling him all morning, but it was too early to be hearing some dumb shit. Ed wasn't a morning person at all, so he planned to call him later.

Tecca's building was in the back, next to the playground and basketball court, in the projects.

When he parked, Tecca's tall lanky body popped out with a corner store bag in his hand, looking mad as usual.

Tecca had a nickname, which was Angry Bird, because he was always pissed off about something.

"What's up, dawg?" Tecca said with his deep tone.

"Damn, fool, where you been at?" Ed asked, looking in the bag, realizing it looked a little short.

Ed hated math and adding, but he knew when money was short and looked funny.

"Laying low, bruh. Shit been hot over here. The feds snatched up like twenty niggas from da hood the other day," Tecca said, shaking his head.

"Fuck all dat shit, bruh. Why this shit look short?"

"Huh," Tecca shot back.

"Nigga, I know this ain't all of it, right here." Ed looked in the bag, and then at Tecca.

Ed gave him eight bricks of coke and told Tecca to bring him fifty percent back.

"The feds got two of my workers and I took a big loss."

"What da fuck that got to do with me?" Ed was starting to get pissed off.

Tecca knew Eddy was a live wire, especially when it came to his money, family or not.

"Give me a few days and I got you, cuz," Tecca said.

"Ight, I got you," Ed replied, knowing his cousin knew he didn't play when it came to money.

"What's up with Jason? I heard niggas on his line," Tecca said.

"Damn. Who want him?"

"Lil Hiss."

"Oh shit. That nigga, Kanye crazy," Ed said, knowing how Lil Hiss got down. If a nigga had beef with him, then they would always pop up dead.

"Yeah, I think they said Jason set Durk up, from Stone Mountain, with some bitch who did bruh in," Tecca said.

"Damn, I gotta holla at bro." Ed's mind went to Ashanti.

"Facts, but I gotta babysit. Hit me later, bro." Tecca got out, leaving him thinking.

***

Zone 3, Atlanta

Outside of Summerhill projects was a hotel, behind a Texaco gas station, which everybody went to on a daily basis because it was cheap.

Apple and RiRi sat in the hotel room, smoking big blunts full of wood and sniffing coke, something they did almost every Friday.

The day Top Shot got killed, that was RiRi's work. She'd proudly set that up, with no remorse.

"You're the daddy," RiRi stated, putting her head in his lap, high out her mind.

"I want you to go get an abortion, love," Apple said, looking at her with his green eyes. Apple was a light skin, pretty boy nigga, with green eyes, from Zone 3. His mom was white and his dad was black and Spanish.

Coke Girlz

He worked for Coral and had a little money, but it was cheap change to Coral. When RiRi told him about some niggas inquiring about him, he made her play it cool and line the lick up.

With RiRi being pregnant, he did not need her anymore. Her pussy was loose and she had a mean head and throat game.

"Abortion? Nigga, you playing? I'm not getting rid of-"

Her words were cut short by a slap to the face from Apple. This wasn't his first time hitting her, so she didn't appear shocked.

"Bitch, you finna do what I tell ya," Apple said before the hotel room door got kicked open and Style rushed in with an AR pistol that took 223 bullets.

Tat. Tat. Tat. Tat. Tat. Tat. Tat.

Style shot Apple and RiRi both, making their bodies spin backwards on the hotel mattress. Style got up close and fired four shots apiece into their domes for his boy, Top Shot, who would've done the same for him, if he was gone.

Coke Girlz

Chapter 29

Downtown, Atlanta

Ashanti and Alex went out to see a new movie at the AMC Theater to get a little time together, since shit had been rocky for them both lately.

The dark movie theater was half full and a little cold inside, so Ashanti put her new Louis Vuitton sweater to use.

Alex had being seeing her with a bunch of new shit lately, but he'd been keeping it to himself, not trying to sound like a dickhead. He knew she wasn't dancing anymore, but he couldn't help but wonder where she was getting money from.

Like any man would, he assumed she was getting it from another nigga.

"Babe, can I ask you something?" Alex asked.

"What's that, baby?" Ashanti watched the movie while listening.

"How are you getting all this shit?' Alex asked, flicking her eye ring.

"What the fuck you mean?" Ashanti got on defensive mode.

She knew this question was eventually coming up, but not right now, on their date.

"I'm just saying, I feel like you cheating on me. I don't even see you no more. And when I do, you rocking new shit," Alex said. A few people looked back at them, trying to watch the movie.

"You calling me a hoe, Alex? I never cheated on your broke ass." she was pissed off now. Ashanti could've done him wrong so many times, but she chose not to because she really did love him. Her loyalty ran deep for people she loved.

"I'm just saying," he said.

"Saying what, Alex? Just because I'm not under you all day don't mean I ain't loyal," she stated.

"So how are you getting all this shit?" he asked.

"None of your fucking business."

"It's like that, shawty?" Alex replied, with an evil grin.

123

"Alex, you tripping," she said, sucking her teeth.

"Your friend, GiGi, tripping," he laughed, but Ashanti wasn't playing now.

Ashanti and GiGi used to be cool, but she was on some snake shit, trying to fuck Alex behind her back.

"What about GiGi?" Ashanti said.

"She got some good pussy," Alex said nonchalantly. An older lady a few seats down heard their whole conversation. She was shaking her head at how shady Alex was.

"So you fucked her?"

"Yep, and she paid my phone bill. You don't give me no attention," Alex said, seeing Ashanti's eyes get glossy. He could tell he hurt her, but he had to be honest.

Ashanti grabbed her soda cup, opened the lid, and tossed it all over his face and upper body. Then she got up and walked off.

Alex sat there, feeling dumb. He regretted hurting her because he knew deep down Ashanti was a good girl and a ride or die. He knew with time she'd be back, sooner than later.

***

Stone Mountain, Georgia

Jason rode through a certain section of Stone Mountain in an Impala on 26-inch rims, a hooked up car he only brought out once in a blue moon to stunt. Shit had been real good for him. Money was flowing and niggas were starting to respect his hand. The whole city knew he killed Durk now. It was the talk of the street.

He knew his girlfriend, India, was up to no good when he overheard her on the phone with one of her girls, talking about Chad, her ex.

Jason tailed India for two days, acting like he was out of town, to put her in his trap.

This morning, Ed called him, talking about a nigga, Lil Hiss. Jason knew who the man was, and he didn't care. Word was there was $100,000 on Jason's head. He told Ed that didn't bother him.

Coke Girlz

He was glad to have official niggas, like Ed, on his team, who gun blasted on any op or potential threats.

Jason stopped at the post office, about to park, until he saw a car ease up on the side of him. When he saw two gunmen slide out of the Cadillac truck with sticks, he pushed on the gas, but bullets shattered the car windows.

Boc. Boc. Boc.

Tat. Tat. Tat. Tat. Tat. Tat.

Jason hit a car, trying to get away from rapid gun fire, as glass landed on his neck and upper back.

"Bitch ass niggas," Jason shouted, as he bent the corner and sped up the block, on a main street.

Jason knew there were projects next to the post office that Durk and his crew used to run. He knew he was slacking, not being on point. Jason had a plan to come back later, when it got dark, and light up the whole projects, whoever was outside.

Chapter 30

Southside, Atlanta

Lil Hiss waited in the waffle house for an old friend to arrive, so they could talk. Having to hear his goons missed their target the other day didn't sit well with him.

Jason was the only person on his mind, since his brother's death. He'd even forgotten about his social life. His babies' mothers had been tripping about him spending time with his children.

Li Hiss disliked beef nowadays because it brought too many downfalls, mainly heat from the feds and local police departments.

Hustling in the Atlanta inner city area was a gamble, so Lil Hiss locked shit down in Clayton County, Alpharetta, Macon, and DeKalb County, while Durk had Stone Mountain.

The man of the hour finally walked in, with a slow smooth bop.

"Lil Hiss, good to see you, big dog. How's everything?" Mills said.

"Maintaining, bruh. Thanks for coming out," Lil Hiss said, as Mills sat down, getting comfortable, and noticing the place was half empty.

Lil Hiss and Mills went a long way back to when Mills used to supply him. Back then, Lil Hiss was on a come up in the game, but now he was almost on the same level as the man sitting across from him.

"Sorry to hear about Durk. He was a good kid, bruh." Mills had heard about Durk's death, and his heart went out to Lil Hiss.

There were so many different rumors about Durk's death, a chick set him up, Jason killed him, police killed him, and the last one, Durk killed himself over a chick.

"That's why I called you out, shawty, because this nigga Jason killed him, or had him killed. Either way, I'm on his ass."

"Jason?" Mills knew who he was talking about. Everybody knew Jason fucked with Buzz, and word in the streets was he was running around slumping shit.

"Yeah. He Buzz people," Lil Hiss stated.

"I know."

"I think, if we come together, we can take over the city and ex out the ops, once and for all." Lil Hiss didn't want to seem thirsty by telling him he needed his help.

Lil Hiss had shooters, but he knew with Mills' help, they would get the job done.

"I'm down, bruh. But first we need to come up with a few plots because I've been trying to get at Buzz for a while now, but he keep sliding through the cracks of my hands."

"Ight. That's the easy part. But what's up with Lil Mills?" Lil Hiss asked about his brother.

"He doing him, pimpin' hard. He back in forth to Cashville and N.C. You know he love that pimp game," Mills laughed.

"Fo sho." Lil Hiss and Mills chopped it up for a few more minutes before leaving, going separate ways.

***

Lenox Mall, Atlanta

Franchesca was in the mall, waiting on her best friend she hadn't see in months. Last night, she called her girl up so they could do some shopping and gossip about the new events in their lives.

Mills went to Albany, Georgia to look at some land because he wanted to build a home for his mom and grandmom soon.

Things had been going well in her love life because Mills did everything to make sure she was well taken care of. Franchesca had a secret she'd been waiting to tell Mills. She was starting to feel like it was the right time to speak on it because Mills kept talking about kids.

Franchesca had a son that her mom and older sister had been raising since she was eighteen years old. The child's father was killed by a young kid named Ed. She knew who killed her baby's daddy because she was right there in the parking lot when Ed and her child's father got into a big argument over some owed money.

Her girl walked up from behind, scaring her.

Coke Girlz

"What's up, bitch? I miss you," Elisa said, hugging her close friend.

Elisa and Franchesca had been friends since the second grade. They talked about everything, but Elisa wasn't going to tell her about her new lifestyle.

"You look like money, bitch. Dripping in double's," Franchesca stated.

"Chanel swag, baby." Elisa showed off her new outfit and purse, everything Chanel.

"What's been going on with you? I don't even see you on social media no more. What's up with that?"

"I have been dealing with a NBA player," Elisa lied. She hated lying to her girl, but she had to.

"What team he play for?"

"He overseas, but enough about me. What's up with you? Who you sucking?" Elisa asked, making her laugh.

"A big baller." Franchesca went on to her tell everything about Mills as they walked through the mall, shopping.

Chapter 31

East Side, Atlanta

Ashanti came out to club Da Libra on the East Side of the city. She came out to get some fresh air and have a few drinks, while putting some plans together.

Since breaking up with Alex, she'd been trying to get her mind right. With Alex being the only man she loved, it was a little harder than she thought to let go.

Buzz told her he had something for her, so she was going to meet him across town the following day.

She thought back to dude she'd met in Miami named Heat. But when she called, his phone went to voicemail, so she gave up on him.

Her girl, Sammy, called, hoping to link up with her sometime this week to kick it. But Ashanti didn't have play time, she had bills to pay.

With shopping, bills, and living a fly life, her stash was running low, very low, so she knew soon she would be hunting for her own vics, instead of waiting on Buzz every time.

Sitting in the back, she saw Style walk into the club with another dude. Her and Style had always been cool. They had a real brother and sister bond.

She saw him come up from the dirt. He was a young nigga, but he knew how to get money in every lane. Recently, before her and his brother, Alex, broke up, Alex told her what type of shit Style was into.

Ashanti got up and walked over to him as her plan started to come together, nice and smooth.

"Style," she said, seeing him smile and his friend just stare at her titties, which were sitting nice in her top, exposing almost all of her breasts.

"Hey, sis. What you doing here?" Style asked, ordering a drink.

The club wasn't full and he'd just come out because his friend girl was the bottle girl. He came to get her car keys so they could use her car to slide on some ops.

"I'm trying to speak to you in private real quick," she shot back, looking at his ugly friend.

"I'll be back," Style's friend said. He'd gotten the clue and was jealous of how his boy walked in the club and already had bad bitches on his dick.

"What's going on? I heard what happened to you and my goofy ass brother," Style laughed, already knowing the news because Alex came home crying to him.

"I don't want to talk about him." She sat down next to him.

Style looked at her like she was crazy because he wasn't about to fuck Alex's leftovers, even though he'd heard her shit was fire.

"I don't rock like that," he said, making her laugh.

"Not in a million years. I got a proposition for you, but our business is between us," Ashanti said, as a few shots came.

"Proposition?" he looked lost.

"Yes. I got five keys of good coke for you, and we finna split it 50/50. A key is going for 35,000 right now, but I trust you," she said.

Style couldn't believe his ears. He wanted to ask where she got it from because this wasn't even her field, but he knew sometimes it was better to leave shit alone.

"When?"

"Whenever you ready," she spat back.

"Damn. I always wondered how you was able to ride in a Benz and put Alex in a position, too. I know dancing ain't do it," Style said, taking a sip of his drink.

"You'll be surprised, playa."

"I got a crew in College Park, East Point, and a few other hoods, trying to get money, so this will be easy," he told her.

"I trust you."

"When I'm done, will you have more? I'm sure, if it's good, people will buy it up," he stated.

Coke Girlz

Ashanti thought for a second before answering. She did want to stay consistent with the product, with the way they both would be winning. She knew if her next robbery didn't consist of finding drugs, she would have to get product from her Uncle Buzz. She knew he would charge her the going rate, as he did other people. He was shady like that, and greedy.

"Next time you will have to pay thirty apiece. I'm just putting you on your feet now," she told him.

"That's fair. I won't let you down. Trust me, shawty, you really fucking with me. I got you Ashanti."

"Fair enough. I'll meet you in da morning in College Park, near the old park, by the dumpster, at 10:20. A bag will be there for you. Get the bag and drive away. Then text me when you done." She loved the way she sounded like a true boss bitch.

"Ight." Style was excited. He'd never even had a whole key. Now Ashanti was about to flood him with five keys.

Ashanti walked out of the club to see people were starting to come now, at midnight.

She saw a handsome, dark skin brother, with gold teeth hop out of a new Bentley truck with two big bodyguards.

Ashanti strutted past the truck, hearing someone shout at her.

"Ay, shawty, hold on," the man she saw get out of the luxury car ran down on her in the middle of the street.

"Shawty, got a name," Ashanti said, as she continue to walk across the street, with him by her side.

"I'm sorry. I had to get your attention. I'm Coral, and whenever you free, I just want to spend some time with you, show you how a real king get down," Coral said, making her giggle and stop on the sidewalk.

"Ok. Give me your number, King," she said, mocking him. Coral gave her his number and she walked off rudely.

"Wait, I ain't get your name?" he shouted.

"You might not," she replied, getting in her car and driving off.

133

Coke Girlz

Chapter 32

College Park, Georgia

Candra woke up in her old room at her mom's house, tired as hell because she hadn't gotten there until 2am.
Her school was out for two weeks, so everybody went home. Some of her friends flew to New York, LA, Texas, Miami, and Chicago, going home. She was lucky she lived in the Atlanta area.
Megan was at work, so she had the house to herself. Candra had plans to get with Jason later, but she couldn't get in touch with Ashanti, for some reason.
She knew Ashanti moved on, but she really wanted to make sure her sister was good. Jason said she was, but she felt a little different because it looked funny. Ashanti used to always be on social media going crazy, with over a million followers. Now she was barely on it.
Candra got herself together so she could focus on her day. Aliana lived in Buckhead, a rich section of town, and she was coming to get her in her dad's Rolls-Royce, in a few. They planned to go out and have a blast.

***

East Point, Georgia

Style and four of his close peers from Zone 1, Zone 3, and Zone 4, were all posted up in Style's side bitch's crib, looking at the four keys. Mostly everybody in the room was a robber or killer, and a part time drug dealer.
"I'ma give everybody a key. I want y'all to bust it down to nicks, dimes, ounces, whatever. Just have mines when it's time, bruh," Style said to the room.
"My hood got a drought right now because Mills outta town," the oldest nigga in the room said. He was twenty-seven years old.
"That's good. Let's run it up. Get at me when y'all done," Style said. Everybody placed their keys in a bag and left.

Style went to pick up the drugs that morning, and everything was there, as Ashanti said it would be. He kept one brick in the trunk, just in case shit went wrong somehow. He felt like this could be a big start if Ashanti stayed consistent.

While he sat down thinking, a thick brown skin woman walked up in a robe with nothing under it, ready to fuck before going to work. He was ready.

***

Douglas High School, Atlanta

"Let me get this right, Buzz. You want me and him to run in the dude crib, rob him, and kill him?" Ashanti asked to make sure she'd heard him right. He'd just told her and Ed to rob a local, big time dealer named Kobe.

They were behind a high school at 11pm, dressed in all black, ready to put in some work.

"Yes, this is an easy job. That's why I put you two on this as a team. But I gotta go. Have fun, kids," Buzz said, turning to leave.

"Hold on. What do I get outta this?" she asked.

"Half," Buzz said.

"What about him?" Ashanti pointed at Ed.

"Shit, he good. He going at his own freewill, baby gurl. Be safe," Buzz said with a laugh, thinking Ed was drummer than he looked.

When Buzz pulled off, they got in Ed's rental car, looking at the piece of paper with the addy on it.

Ed drove in silence, already knowing the address by heart. Buzz wanted Ashanti and her crew to go on the lick, but Eddy refused. He told him he would go because he was a real killer. Word on the street was that the dope was he was using had gotten the best of him.

Kobe and Buzz had hated each other for years. Kobe used to be a big time brick layer.

Now, Kobe's son, Coral, was the man, and Buzz disliked that, also.

Coke Girlz

Ashanti kept quiet, not trying to really talk because she had an attitude. She was horny and annoyed.

When they got to Dill Ave in Zone 3, he parked across the street from a yellow house. Ed pulled out two twin desert eagle handguns, and passed her one.

"I got one. Let's hurry up," she said, pulling out a Glock 19 with an extended clip and getting out the car.

"This bitch crazy," Ed said, following her to the back of the house, wondering what she was trying to do.

***

Kobe and two younger women, in their twenties, were sniffing heroin on the table in the kitchen, dancing to the music, all high as a kite. Kobe found the women on Fulton Industrial, a hoe stroll where he loved buying hookers.

Living with HIV for the last ten years made him not give a fuck about life itself. He used to be big time. He sold dope all over Atlanta. He used to make a millions every week, until he caught a ten year bid, when his son was a kid.

Coming home, his life went down the drain when he started getting high on dog food. When he heard of his old ops, like Buzz, doing good, he hated himself more.

His son, Coral, took good care of him. He needed nothing. He was plugging his son into his old clients and letting him use his home as a stash house.

Kobe pulled his pants down, after taking another hit, and let one of the woman give him a blow job, while the other woman danced around.

Seconds later, Kobe felt cold steel to the back of his head. He opened his eye, while the woman was still sucking his dick, deep throating. She was so high, she didn't see the two intruders.

"Get the fuck up," Ed said, turning down the music and admiring the snow-bunny's head game.

"Who the fuck are y'all bitches?" Kobe said.

"Turn around and find out," Ashanti said, with her gun to his head.

The other woman wasn't dancing anymore. She was holding on to her friend, scared to death.

"You come to suck my dick, too?" Kobe asked Ashanti with a smirk, as he turned up the music.

Bloc. Bloc. Bloc. Bloc. Bloc. Bloc.

Ashanti killed both of the two hookers as Kobe's face got serious. He knew whoever they were, they were there to kill.

"Where is everything stashed at?" Ed asked, turning the music back down.

"Just kill me. I've been waiting to meet Allah for a long time." Kobe's words were genuine.

"Where are the drugs?" Ashanti asked.

"Fuck y'all," Kobe said, running to the living room to get the SK Assault rifle he had for times like this.

Boom.
Boom.
Boom.
Boom.
Boom.
Boom.

Ed's bullets landed directly in the middle of the old man's back, killing him instantly.

"Split up so we can find this shit," Ed told Ashanti, as he went upstairs, stepping over dead bodies.

Ashanti started searching the kitchen, living room, and hallway closet, but then something made her lift up the floor mat. When she lifted the mat she saw a piece of wood that had a red string sticking out. She lifted it, and the wood easily popped up, and other pieces of the floor loosened and came out.

When she saw the money and drugs, she yelled.

"Found it," she shouted.

Ed came down, seconds later, with nothing, to see her pulling out money and drugs from the floor.

When he went to help her, they both bumped heads. Then something happened. They looked at each other in the eyes and started to kiss passionately.

Coke Girlz

They tongued each other down for close to three minutes, about to fuck right there. They were so caught up in moment.

"Wait," he said.

"What?" She'd wanted him badly, ever since she first laid eyes on him, but she had a man.

"Let's get out of here and go back to my place," he said, getting up and looking for bags to place the money and drugs in, so they could leave.

After a minute of bagging up the earnings, they made it out safely and went to Ed's crib.

In the car, Ashanti was playing with his dick the whole ride, even sucking it and playing with his balls. He even fingered her tight drenched coochie.

As soon as they made it to his bedroom, they were fucking all over the place. It was the best sex she'd ever had because Ed knew how to make love to her and hit her G-spot. Ashanti climaxed over five times in less than forty minutes. She was head over heels.

Romell Tukes

Coke Girlz

Chapter 33

Downtown, Atlanta

Ashanti woke up the next morning to breakfast in bed, still at Ed's crib. His bedroom was large, and set up nicely. She was overwhelmed. Her body still felt she was on cloud nine.

"I hope you hungry," Ed said, standing over her with a tray of food, wearing Gucci boxers, showing his well-defined body.

"Yesss," she said smiling, seeing a piece of her track on the floor. Ed saw it, too, making him laugh.

"Well, that's not mines," he said laughing with her.

"You play play, huh?" She took the tray, sitting up to eat and thinking about how good the dick was last night.

"Can I be real?" he asked.

Ashanti thought he was going to say the sex was trash or something, so she got nervous.

"What?"

"How you wanna go about this because I do like you, and that pussy gonna drive a nigga crazy," he said, making her blush like a little kid.

"I don't really know, Eddy. We both stuck in the field. Do we even have time for a relationship?" she asked, enjoying the sunny side up eggs and bacon he'd made for her.

"Only time will tell, so I guess you can say we dating."

"I can accept, babe," she replied.

"So I'm babe now?" Ed asked.

"Shit, the way you was hitting that pussy, you babe, babe, for real, for real," she said, making him crack up laughing.

Ed had no idea she was this cool, down to earth, and funny. When he first saw her at the club, he thought she was just another stuck up bad bitch, out to snake niggas out of their bag.

"What's your goals, shawty? I know you don't plan on robbing niggas forever because that's a dangerous game," he said, looking into her eyes.

"I just want to be good, finally stable, you know," she shot back.

"You have to invest, Ashanti. You can't save money when you blowing money," he gave her game.

"I know, but I got some things in the making," she said.

Ashanti didn't know Ed well enough to tell him about her drug dealing or plans to be number one queen-pen of the city.

"That's cool, but don't trust Buzz. He's only using you. I shouldn't be telling you this, but I'm down with you," he told her, seeing she had an unfazed look.

"You kill for him, so you must trust him enough?" she asked.

"I don't trust him. I trust the position he put me in. it's about a bag with me." Ed saw his phone ringing.

"I just look like this, Ed. I knew what type of snake my uncle was before dealing with him. He a snake, but I'm a double headed snake, with venom." She wanted him to know she was on point.

"Ok. I'm here for you, but I have to bust a few moves," he said, looking at his phone.

"I'm coming." She got out of bed to get dressed.

"Huh?" he wasn't used to making runs with other people. He didn't need a witness.

"Damn. You must be going to see other bitches," she said, looking at him.

Automatically, red flags went up in his head. He knew it was too good to be true. Bad bitch, great sex, and her own money, he knew she was crazy.

Ed didn't know what to say as all types of thoughts filled his head. When he heard Ashanti laughing, he looked at her.

"Ed, I'm not that type of girl. You're a man. You're gonna do what you do. Just know who number one is." She kissed his lips, grabbing his manhood and getting him aroused.

They started fucking on the bed for half an hour. Then they got ready to leave.

***

College Park, Georgia

Coke Girlz

Ed drove Ashanti to a hair store near her mom's crib so she can buy some tracks.

Ashanti was going to her mom's house to spend some time with Candra, who had texted her new number, which Jason gave her.

"I'll be in and out," Ashanti said, getting out of the car and running inside the store, only to run into Alex coming out. Ashanti's face had a big smile since last night, until now.

"You don't answer your phone for a nigga, huh?" Alex said, looking upset.

"Alex, I'm past that. We don't have shit to talk about."

"It's like that?" Alex replied.

"Facts."

"I need you, Ashanti. I can't live without you, baby. Please, I'll do anything," he broke down.

"Alex, it's over. Move on. Get over it. You fucked up."

"I'm sorry. Please give me a chance. I fucked up," he said.

"I moved on. I have to go." Ashanti walked off, but Alex grabbed her arm.

"Don't play with me," Alex said, as his eyes turned red.

"What are you talking about? Let my arm go, Alex."

"Bitch, you not going nowhere, until I say," he demanded.

"I don't want you, Alex. It's fucking over. Get help." she tried to snatch her arm back, but he had a hold on her so tight that her arm turned red.

Alex slapped Ashanti so hard that her body flew onto the floor. Alex was about to start swinging on her in the doorway of the hair store.

Bloc. Bloc. Bloc.

Three bullets hit Alex in his lower back, making him collapse on to the store floor. When Ashanti saw he was shot, she got up, and Eddy had a smoking gun.

"Touch her again, I'll kill you, fuck nigga," Eddy told Alex, who was crying in pain.

Ed and Ashanti got in his rental car and raced off, without saying a word. Ashanti didn't want Ed to kill Alex because he wasn't

143

worth it. But she did realize she left money and drugs at his crib, but she knew it was safe.

Coke Girlz

Chapter 34

East Side, Atlanta

Megan had just got done spending most of her day with her daughter, Candra, who'd been home for the holidays. Having Candra around made things so easy for her. Yesterday Ashanti came by her crib to check on Candra and things got real confrontational between her and Ashanti because she didn't want her in her home.

Driving to work, Megan had four new iPhones in her purse, and five balloons full of drugs that she was sneaking in for Mell.

Megan never thought she would be bringing contraband into the jail for an inmate, but Mell's dick was so good that whatever he wanted, she was going to aid him. She planned to do a double shift tonight, and call Mell out to pick up trash around the yard, so she could take him into a janitor's closet and let him fuck the soul out of her.

Since getting dicked out the right way, she'd been happy and on another cloud, out of this world.

She had her own parking spot, outside of the jail, next to a big pickup truck her boss drove. Megan's heart was racing. She prayed she didn't get caught bringing all this shit in, especially the drugs.

The phones, she could make a dumb excuse for. But the drugs, she knew it was over. She saw female officers get walked off the compound, at least four to six times a month.

Megan took a deep breath and went to work, hoping for the best, scared to death.

***

Zone 4, Atlanta

Style was in the West End area, making big moves with Top Shot's older brother, Real, who was a known getting money cat, who busted his gun also.

"We about to get money, Style. You came through at the right time. This half of key finna be gone by tomorrow, bruh. I got some people already trying to cop it tonight. I hope you got more," Real asked Style, who was rolling a blunt of good weed to smoke to the head.

Style had just given Real five hundred grams of his last key. He only had a half of joint left in the cut.

He chose to put Real on because he knew he was solid, just like Top Shot was before he got killed on their drill.

"I'll have more, bro. God damn, you just got half," Style said, banking on Ashanti's word.

His crew was almost done with the product he gave them. They told him the drugs were moving like hot cakes, and the fiends loved it.

"Ight. But aye, shawty, on some real shit, bruh, thank you for taking care of that Apple situation. If you ain't do it, then I would've," Real said.

"I know. But I did what I was supposed to do."

"On everything, bruh," Real said, thinking about his little brother.

Style had heard his brother, Alex, was in the hospital after being shoot. But Style didn't really give a fuck about it, at all.

Style hated pussies, like Alex, family or not. He didn't respect sucker niggas.

***

Zone 1, Atlanta

Mills had a few workers in Kya Heights projects. One was his big cousin, Snoopy, who was five years older than him, and shady.

Mills knew Snoopy was a snake. But he knew he had to keep a few snakes close by, just in case.

Today he was picking up money, and tomorrow he would have his boy, Fats, drop off the product to his workers all over the city.

Coke Girlz

Teaming up with Lil Hiss was a good look. The more, the better, but he wasn't so worried about his ops at the moment. He was on a bag.

He pulled into the back of the hood, where it was pitch black and empty, just full of cars.

Mills called Snoopy, and got the voicemail, but he saw him coming out of one of the buildings. Then he got out of his Lexus truck.

Mills wondered why he didn't see no bag in his cousin's hands, and why he did not come alone, like he always did.

The smirk on Snoopy's face said it all, as he got closer to Mills. Something told Mills to look behind him, and when he did, he saw Buzz and his shooters. It was a setup.

Tat. Tat. Tat. Tat. Tat. Tat.

Mills ran for his life, dodging behind cars and avoiding gunfire. Mills ran across the street, trying to save himself.

When he made it clear and out of sight, he made a few calls for someone to come get him. He couldn't believe his own blood tried to set him up. He saw it all over Snoopy's face, the betrayal.

Romell Tukes

Coke Girlz

Chapter 35

Grady Memorial Hospital, Atlanta

Alex laid in the cold hospital room, trying to hold back his manly tears.

Being shot in his lower back damaged his lower spine, killing a lot of big nerves, making him paralyzed for life. The doctors were lucky to save his life, but now he would spend the rest of his life in a wheelchair.

He'd been in the hospital for a few days, with a shit bag, thinking about how he should've kept walking. But he tried to make things work between him and Ashanti.

Deep down, he knew he shouldn't have put his hands on her, but he was caught up in the moment.

Alex had never been shot, and he really hated Ashanti for it. He knew who the dude was who shot him because he'd seen him a few times at his job. He used to fuck with one of his co-workers.

He hated both of them, and vowed to get them back.

There was a light knock at the room door, and then a pretty, small, white woman walked in.

"Excuse me, sir, but you have visitors," the nurse said, as two cops walked in, dressed in plain clothes.

Alex saw a white cop and an older, black, heavy set woman, with a cute face, playing with keys.

"Mr. Alex, glad you made it," the woman said, sitting down and putting on her cop face, as the nurse left the room.

"Thank you. But who are you?" Alex asked, looking at her legs move freely and thinking about his.

"I'm Detective Halls, and this is my partner, Mike, for short," the woman said. She was known detective from Bankhead. Detective Hall was a vicious cop. She was one of the worst in the city.

"We here to find out what happened," Mike finally spoke up.

"I was shot," Alex got smart.

"Of course, you're in a wheelchair. You can't walk. We just trying to figure out who you pissed off," Detective Halls said, with her evil grin.

"A woman named Ashanti and a dude name Ed," Alex snitched. Both of the cops looked at each other like they hit the jackpot.

"Eddy, huh? You must be a drug dealer, or something, if Ed shot you. I'm surprised you still here," Mike said, knowing Ed real well. The whole Atlanta PD knew him. He was their top five most wanted in the city, for a few unsolved murders.

"I ain't do shit," Alex shouted, unable to move his lower body.

"Write us a statement, and we will look into it," Detective Halls said, handing him a form and pen to write statements.

"Your fingers work, right?" Mike joked, as they got a good laugh right off Alex, as he wrote a statement on Ashanti and Ed.

"You guys are very funny, I see," Alex said.

"Hold on. I saw you with Style before," Mike said, remembering he'd seen Alex a few weeks ago at a car wash, talking to Style and Top Shot. Mike was watching Top Shot and waiting to arrest him for a double murder charge from last year.

"That's my brother."

"Ain't that some shit?" Detective Hall said.

"Is he ok?" Alex asked, sounding concerned, but he was really trying to be nosey.

"No, he's not. I'm waiting on his downfall, him and his little crew. But it just hit me, you have bigger problems to worry about," Detective Halls said, as she made eye contact with Mike, who already knew where this was going.

"Me? How?" Alex didn't understand her comment.

"We found two guns and two hundred grams of dope in your car," Detective Halls stated.

"What? I don't have no guns. I never saw dope in my life, or sold it. I been living off a woman. Y'all have the wrong person. Maybe it was the wrong car." Alex started talking fast. He was so scared.

"We got the correct person, trust us. Now it's on you if you want to roll around in a wheelchair in prison, or free. You already

Coke Girlz

snitched, so you will be fresh fish on the line, when you get to Fulton County Jail," Mike added, seeing fear in Alex's eyes.

Alex had never been to jail, and he was scared to go, especially being in a wheelchair. He knew he would be dead meat.

"What do you want?" Alex gave in.

"Style. Has he ever admitted to any murders, or are attempted murders?" Detective Halls knew he would fall for the trap. Truth was, they had nothing on Alex, at all. He was an easy vic to build a case on Style, who they'd been looking at.

"Yeah, I know about two he told me about," Alex said.

"Write it all down, while we record you," Mike said, pulling out a snitch form and a tape recorder.

***

Zone 6, Atlanta

Coral had been running around all day. It was the 3rd of the month and he'd been picking up money and dropping off work all around Atlanta, since 10am.

He had one more pick up, then he was going to his grandma's house, who had raised him since he was nine years old.

His youngin, Apple, had recently been killed, which hit his pockets hard. But he knew it was part of the game. Before Apple's death, he told him a little nigga named Top Shot was trying to rob him, but he was going to slide on him first. Coral had a feeling the plan would backfire. Plus, he knew Apple wasn't focused because he was getting high.

He parked on Moreland Ave, waiting on Stacks to arrive with his money. He got a call from an unfamiliar number and answered the phone.

"Who speaking?" he answered, placing the call on the car speaker.

"Hey, this KiKi, the female you stopped outside the Club Da Libra, almost two weeks ago," the female said, who really was Ashanti.

"Oh yes, the sexy woman, who wouldn't give me her name. So, I finally get it, KiKi," Coral said, feeling a hard on just thinking about her.

"I'm KiKi, but what you up to?"

"Just taking care of some business. But I was hoping to meet up with you, whenever you free," Coral said, seeing Stacks come to the car window with a big duffle bag and tossing it into the passenger side window.

"How about tonight?" Ashanti said.

"What time and where?"

"I'll text you everything as soon as I get off work," she said.

"Perfect, and wear something sexy," Coral said.

"Always, daddy," Ashanti said before she hung up.

Coral loved her soft voice. He couldn't wait to see what KiKi's pussy was like.

Chapter 36

Zone 6, Atlanta

"I wonder how many pickups this nigga did," Faith asked in the driver's seat of her cousin's Honda. She'd borrowed it this morning for their mission.

Ashanti had just hung up the phone with Coral, as they tailed him all through the city.

"Fuck that. I just want to know how much he got in them bags," Ashanti stated, watching Coral speed through Zone 6, most likely getting ready for their date.

"He a thirsty nigga. But thanks for that money this morning. How you come across that?" Faith asked, thinking about all the paper Ashanti brought to her crib.

"My people put me on to some shit at the last minute. But we finally starting to climb the ladder," Ashanti said, texting her boo, Ed.

"Elisa said one of her ex-boyfriends is doing big things, but she don't want to line him up. She wants someone else to do it. So I was thinking maybe you can use them stripper chicks you told us about." Faith made a left, hopping on the highway, trying to keep a distant eye on Coral.

"That's no problem. They'll be down. But Elisa been acting funny lately," Ashanti stated.

"Home girl got some real issues. I just found out the bitch take meds and all," Faith said, shaking her head.

"What makes you think that?" Ashanti asked, knowing Elisa had a lot of issues from her upbringing and childhood.

"I saw her bugging this morning, when I went to drop off her money," Faith said.

"How was she acting?" Ashanti kept an eye on Coral's car.

"Talking to herself, as if I wasn't even there. But crazy part is, she popped some pills and the bitch went right back to regular," Faith said.

"I ain't know she was tripping like that. But regardless, she's our cousin and she loyal to us, so that's all that really matters," Ashanti said, as Coral pulled into a nice middle class neighborhood outside the ghetto.

"He getting out," Faith said, parking on the corner.

"We about to make our move. It's now or never," Ashanti said, pulling out a gun and slowly exiting the car.

***

Coral had been using his grandmom's home, which he'd bought her, as a stash house, since the death of his father, Kobe. His grandmom was an OG. She used to be down with a vicious crew in the 1960s and 1970s, killing shit. She was a Black Panther still, to this day.

Being raised by a grandmom, who was a killer and cold hearted, made him want to be the same way. Coral never wanted to be a broke killer. Like most, he started hustling and chasing money.

He rushed into the house with three bags full of money. Coral was going to place it in his stash spot in the hallway closet, behind a small door used for storage.

Checking his watch, he saw he still had time to get fresh before his date. Normally, at this time, his grandmom was sleep.

Coral had new outfits and shoes upstairs, just in case he didn't feel like going back home.

"Don't fucking move," Ashanti said from behind Coral, as he was moving shit out of the closet to stash the bags he had behind him, on the side of the wall.

Faith took the bags and placed them near the stairs.

Coral knew the voice. He'd just gotten off the phone with her.

"KiKi?" Coral stood up, slowly turning around, wishing he'd never left his gun in his car.

"It's Ashanti. But back up and put your hands in the air. Where the money?" He did everything she requested.

This was Coral's first time being robbed and confronted by guns, so he was worried about his welfare and safety.

Coke Girlz

"Everything is in the closet, behind the little door. It's twenty keys and $100,000," Coral said.

"Plus, the money in the bags," Faith said, giving him a wink.

Coral couldn't believe he was really being robbed by two bad bitches.

"When opportunities present themselves, you gotta go for it," Ashanti said before blowing Coral's head off with one shot.

Ashanti quickly crawled into the closet and saw two gym bags and a pillow case, full of money and keys.

While in the closet, Ashanti thought she heard a crack upstairs, as if someone was walking around. Before she could say a word, she heard two loud shotgun blasts.

Boom.

Boom.

"Old bitch," Faith yelled, seeing an old lady, with a shotgun pointed at her, coming downstairs.

The bullets missed and took off a large chunk of the living room wall. When Coral's grandmom heard the gunfire, she woke up and grabbed her shotgun with the double barrel and double action.

When Faith saw the older woman trying to reload the shotgun, she fired three shots into her upper torso, making her fall down the flight of stairs.

Faith stood over Coral's grandmom's body, which was still moving, and shot her in the head.

"Damn, bitch, I'm pretty sure the whole block is awake. Let's go." Ashanti arms were filled with bags.

"That old slut almost killed me," Faith said, getting the bags of money she'd placed near the wall.

"We should've checked the crib first," Ashanti said outside, knowing it could've gotten really ugly a second ago, if Faith wasn't fast on her feet.

"Don't you think, genius?" Faith had an attitude.

Ashanti knew Faith was upset, as always, but she'd almost lost her life because of a mistake they made.

"You're good, and alive, don't be so naïve," Ashanti said, getting into the driver's seat of the car.

"Bitch, naïve? I almost got shot because your dumb ass was in a rush for nothing. I could've easily checked the crib first." Faith was being dramatic.

"So why didn't you, genius?" Ashanti turned up the music, driving off. Ashanti knew how easy it was to hit her buttons, and she loved it.

Coke Girlz

Chapter 37

Elisa woke up in cold sweats from daytime sleep because she was tired as hell. She hadn't gotten any sleep last night. Elisa had been having nightmares again, of horrible things from her past life, which she kept in a bottle.

Only a few people knew a little about her rough life. She'd never told anybody her real story, the whole story.

She suffered from so many disorders and mental health diseases that she couldn't keep up with them. All she knew was to take certain meds to help her deal with life.

The doorbell ringing made her get out of bed and get herself together. She rocked booty shorts and slippers to answer the door.

Ashanti was at the door with a bag of money, smiling, seeing Elisa just woke up.

"Hey, bitch." Ashanti walked in

"What you been doing?" Elisa said, as she let Ashanti all the way inside

"Getting money," Ashanti said.

"I got somebody for us," Elisa said, sitting down.

"Who?"

"An ex of mines," Elisa said, unsure about the whole thing.

Ashanti peeped game. "Whenever you figure it out, let me know. But this is for you," Ashanti poured the money out on the table from Coral's lick.

Ashanti still had the drugs because she had to give her Uncle Buzz some of it.

"Damn. Faith just dropped some money off," Elisa said, overwhelmed at how fast the loot was coming in.

"This is what we on, bitch, getting money. I told you," Ashanti said, happy to see her girl smile.

"How much is this?" Elisa started to count the blue faces.

"Sixty thousand dollars," Ashanti had divided the $180,000 her and Faith gathered from the Coral lick and split it three ways.

"Thanks," Elisa said.

"You're part of the team, girl. You're really gang gang."

"Shut up," Elisa laughed. Her cousin was so goofy at times.

"On some real shit, you know I'm here for you, and you can talk to me about anything," Ashanti said.

"I know."

"You sure?"

"Facts. I'm good, cuz. Now get out so I can take a shower," Elisa told her

"Bye, stanky." Ashanti got up to leave.

***

Southside, Atlanta

Ashanti rushed to her crib to get dressed in her fitness gear so she could meet Sammy, her bestie, at the gym. She hadn't been to the gym in a long time, but she'd been seeing a lot of people embrace fitness lately.

Planet Fitness was in a shopping center next to a pizza store, which she found funny. Ashanti had five thousand dollars in cash in a yellow envelope for Sammy. She saw her Toyota parked in the back, so Ashanti parked her Benz next to it.

Ashanti got out and opened up Sammy's car door to see it was unlocked. She placed the money inside and went for the gym.

As soon as she walked inside, the smell of sweat and musk hit her. All she could think about was who would want to be around people smelling like this.

Sammy was by the dumbbells, lifting ten pound dumbbells in a curl form with her arms.

"You look like you been coming here forever." Ashanti approached her bestie, who wore leggings, showing her toned body and nice ass. She could have been a dancer.

"I love working out, when I have time. Plus, it be some sexy ass niggas up in this bitch," Sammy joked.

"Gurl, you play. But what's up?" Ashanti said, starting to strength train.

Coke Girlz

"Same ole thing, working hard for pennies and struggling. But I know God will guide me," Sammy said.

"How's your brother?"

"Good. It's crazy because after I told you the situation, my little brother's plug came up missing. The nigga, Woop, is big around the city. But Sav is out doing good, working at a fast-food spot," Sammy stated, while working out, seeing a drip of sweat roll down her forehead.

"Sav a good kid." Ashanti tried to downplay what she'd just heard.

"Yeah, but I'm done stripping at them nightclubs. That shit was too much on me, having to find babysitters and spending money. I don't have no babysitters. My own child's father wouldn't even watch his own son if I paid him." Sammy hated her deadbeat baby's father.

"You don't need him. You got me, the godmother. I've been meaning to stop by, but I been having so much going on. OMG," Ashanti said.

"I know. But I need to be honest with you for a second." Sammy stopped working out.

"What's up?"

"I want to get down," Sammy said.

Ashanti tried to give her a dumbfounded look. "What do you mean, girl?"

"Ashanti, I'm not dumb. I know what's really going on," Sammy told her.

"I have no idea what the fuck you talking about," Ashanti said and continued to exercise.

"Really, Ashanti? You finna do me like that, after all we been through? They saying it was some bad bitches who robbed and killed Woop," Sammy said out loud.

"Gurl, you tripping," Ashanti said hoping, nobody else heard her.

"I want to get down," Sammy said, with her hands on her hips.

"Sammy, this ain't what you want. I'm telling you," Ashanti said.

"I'm about da life, and I need money. Ashanti, I'm late on bills and I need help. I have a son."

"I'll give you a shot. Stop talking about it. Let's just work out," Ashanti said.

"Thank you. OMG. I won't let you down, baby girl." Sammy was excited, thinking about her new job.

Chapter 38

Albany, Georgia

Buzz asked Ashanti to meet him at a park near his home, forty minutes away from Atlanta. She was coming with Jason, so he planned to kill two birds with one stone. He had to give Jason twenty-six keys that Jason had already paid for.

Having Ashanti on the team was a big plus. She was taking out all his ops, and he was getting money, at the same time.

Leaning on his truck, drinking a cup of lean, something one of his young boys put him on to, Ed was in Macon, Georgia. He was with his boys, opening up shop out there, and networking, which was something Buzz needed.

Ed and Jason helped make him into the boss he was today. Buzz had been trying to find Mills, but he kept missing his chance. Mills always got away. He put money on Mills' head, and nobody was able to toe tag him yet. But soon, he planned to send Ashanti his way.

Buzz knew Ashanti needed more work before he sent her in the jungle with Mills because he was a vet.

Jason's car pulled up, and Ashanti hopped out in her Fendi sunglass and Fendi print outfit, hugging her body, looking like the Diva she was.

Ashanti grabbed a bag out of the back seat and handed it to Buzz.

"There you go," Ashanti said.

"How many in here?" Buzz asked, as he looked into the bag, knowing wherever she got it from, it was good work.

"That's from Coral. But who do you have in mind?" Ashanti asked, as Buzz handed Jason the bag.

"I owe you 16, Jason. Give me until later. As far as your next lick, there is a man named Big Loot, from Zone 1 that I need you to get at." Buzz handed her a photo with an address on it.

"I'll holla at you when it's done," Ashanti said, walking off. Her ass jiggled loosely because she had on no panties. Buzz didn't look too hard because that was his niece and he didn't want to seem like a pervert.

"Call me when you got the rest of my shit," Jason told Buzz, getting inside his car. Jason knew, firsthand, his uncle was a straight pussy, but he was about his paper.

"Can't trust that nigga," Jason said, getting in the car and driving off.

"Trust is earned," Ashanti said, looking at the pic of Big Loot.

"Facts. But Big Loot should be easy. He be playing in them strip clubs a lot," Jason said, giving Ashanti an idea to call Sayla and Cream.

"Thanks."

"You been stacking money?" he asked.

"Hell yeah and living life. I got a man now. I'm happy. Alex is dead to me." She shook her head, looking out the window as he cruised down the highway, doing the speed limit.

"New boyfriend? Who?"

"Mind your business," she laughed.

"Girl, who is it?"

"Eddy."

"Gunplay Eddy, who work for Buzz?" Jason asked.

"Yeah. And don't go running your mouth," she told him.

Jason couldn't believe it. But he knew what type of nigga Ed was. He stood on morals and honor. Ed was a good, solid dude, so he knew she was straight. He just didn't want her to get hurt.

"As long as you happy."

"I sure am happy. But what's been going on in Stone Mountain, since we took care of Durk?" She asked

"Beef after beef. His older brother, Lil Hiss, is out to get me. But we keep going back and forth," Jason said.

"You need my help?" she asked.

"Hell nah. You gotta worry about your own shit now, sis."

"I got a crew. And I'm getting money on the side. I got Alex's brother, Style, moving work for me," she said.

"I heard of him. But be easy, this drug game is shiesty."

"I know, but it's the risk I wanna take," she told him. They changed conversations, talking about Megan next.

***

Downtown, Atlanta

Ashanti met up with Sayla and Cream to see if they would want to get in on the Big Loot missions she had in store.

It was 4:00am and she was awaiting her girls in the Waffle House, a well-known afterhours spot. Most club hoppers would grab a bite to eat and find the after party, which normally ended in a hotel somewhere.

Ed wanted her to come through, so she was wearing a nice, cute Dolce & Gabbana outfit, with heels.

Ashanti knew how to keep a man. Sex appeal always kept the fire in a relationship lit.

Both Sayla and Cream walked in side by side, laughing like two little high school girls.

Ashanti waved them over to join her, while finishing the egg sandwich she'd been munching on for the last five minutes, waiting on them.

"What's up, girl?" Cream said, hugging Ashanti and checking out her D&G fit.

"Glad y'all here." Ashanti hugged Sayla, too, before sitting back down.

"You looking good. We been waiting on your call," Sayla said.

"I know. I just been busy putting shit together," Ashanti stated.

"You got something for us?" Cream cut straight to the point, playing with her extra-long fingernails.

"Yeah, I do. It's a man named Big Loot," Ashanti said, seeing the women both look at each other.

"Oh, Big Nasty," Cream said.

"No, Big Loot," Ashanti restated.

"Gurl, we call him Big Nasty in the club. He a regular. Me and Cream was just laughing about him because he just vomited all over the VIP section in Magic City," Sayla said.

"I think he had liquor poison," Cream said.

"I don't know, but he threw up on a few dancers. He paid the owner $30,000 for that shit," Sayla said.

"I need y'all to line him for me?" Ashanti asked, looking at both of them.

"Already done. We'll call you in day or so," Sayla stated, as they left Ashanti.

… Coke Girlz

Chapter 39

West Side, Atlanta

Club Blue Flame was turned all the way up tonight. Jason was there celebrating his birthday, drinking with a couple of close friends and having a good time.

With so much beef and drama going on, having fun wasn't an option for him or his crew.

All the sexy naked women sliding up and down the poles and shaking their ass muscles made him realize how much he really missed the club scene.

The club was going up tonight, but Jason was planning to leave with a dancer, who was a famous Instagram model that also shook her ass in the clubs. Her name was Bri Doll.

It was so many people in the club that Jason couldn't spot an op if he wanted to.

The bottle girls brought far more bottles of Ace into their section. Jason popped a few more, and then left the club with Bri Doll under his arm.

"Let's go to the W, baby," Bri Doll said, exiting the club doors with all eyes on her phat ass.

Bri Doll was a cute, brown skin chick, with a short length hairdo, and tats all over her super large booty. But most of all, her tongue was extra-long.

"I'm cool with dat, shawty."

"I hope so because I'm horny. I'ma ride so good tonight. You finna put a ring on this finger," Bri Doll told him, climbing into his car that she liked.

"A ring?" Jason knew she was a thot and a lot of niggas was running inside of her. He'd even heard the rumors of niggas gang-banging her and filming it. One thing he could stamp was her pussy was tight and always wet.

The whole ride to the hotel Bri Doll was in the car mirror, looking at herself. Jason laughed at himself because, without make-up, she wasn't even all that, and she knew it.

It didn't take long to get to the W Hotel, but Jason had been watching a blue SUV tail him since he left the club. Jason had a Glock 30 chrome with a 32-shot clip under his seat.

Pulling into the hotel parking lot, Jason pulled the gun from under the seat and placed it in his lap. When Bri Doll saw this, she automatically got scared, feeling her life was in danger.

"Bitch, if you set me up, I'ma kill your bald head ass," he said, looking in the rearview mirror, seeing someone was on his ass.

"What? I'll never play with you, Jason. What are you about to do?" she asked with fear in her voice.

Jason zoned in on his target, who was on his bumper, and came up with a quick plan, not even listening to Bri Doll babble about nothing in his ear.

He hit the brakes and put the car in reverse, backing up and smashing into the SUV's grill.

Jason jumped out, wasting no time dumping into the SUV.

Bloc.

Bloc.

Bloc.

Bloc.

Bloc.

Bloc.

Bloc.

Bloc.

Jason delivered headshots to both of the shooters in the driver and passenger seats.

Bri Doll started screaming and Jason turned his gun on her, about to fire, until he saw marked and unmarked police cars come from all over the place.

Jason ran through cars at top speed, tossing the murder weapon, hoping to make it to the highway for a getaway.

Six cop cars were on his ass. Jason was so busy looking behind him that he didn't see a car slam into him. Jason's body flew in the air and came down on the hood of a cop car.

Coke Girlz

The cops attacked Jason and started to beat the shit out of him, while placing tight cuffs on him, and taking him away. Bri Doll stood there, crying, as police arrested her too.

***

Zone 3, Atlanta

Zone 3 precinct was where the most likely shady cops were, and the home of Mike, aka Whit Mike, and Dt Halls, aka Big Butt. Those were their names in the streets, to local criminals.

Jason was in the bullpen alone, thinking how did this happen so quickly. He started to wonder if the men he shot in the truck were really his ops, or undercover cops. No matter what, there was no doubt in his mind he was fucked with no type of lube.

"Jason, our man," Dt Halls and her partner yelled as they walked up to the gate, both with big smiles.

"I haven't seen you in a long time," Mike said, with papers in his hands.

"What's the charges?" Jason asked, as he sat down, calm, cool, and collected.

"Oh, man, you fucked, Jason. We got you on four murders," Mike said.

"Four?" Jason was shocked.

"A while back, you fucking killed two New York dudes in broad daylight. We got a few witnesses for that. Then tonight you performed like a true gangster. You killed two men wanted for other crimes," Dt. Halls said, shaking her head.

"Not the birthday gift you planned on?" Mike said.

"Fuck y'all. I ain't do shit," Jason said, holding his ground.

"I hate to tell you, but you really have to worry about us because you're going to Union City Federal Hold Over," Dt. Halls said.

"That's a fed spot?" Jason was a little confused because Union City was a fed jail for federal inmates fighting cases.

"You think four murders was going to the state, so you can beat all charges with a good lawyer, and be home in a few months?" Mike asked.

"Shit." Jason was sick his case went to the feds because niggas don't beat the feds.

"You got some valuable rats you can thank for the feds picking your case up. But you're famous, right? Enjoy your famous high," Dt. Halls said as they laughed, leaving.

Jason was sick. He was down for four murders. He laid down, thinking about what he could've done different.

Coke Girlz

Chapter 40

Austell, Georgia

Sammy had brought her son to Six Flags for his birthday, and she was drained. Not only did Sammy have her son, but he'd brought a gang of his friends along.

She'd just fed the kids and was parked on the bench, resting her feet. There were a few other parents resting, who'd come along with her, and one father she was feeling.

Sammy got the five thousand dollars her girl left for her in the car the last time she saw her, but that wasn't real money.

Since there discussion, she'd been waiting on Ashanti to contact her for a job, so she could get her bag right.

"These kids driving you crazy, too, huh?" a man said, appearing from behind her.

"It shows?" she asked, seeing it was the handsome man with all the expensive jewelry, who'd brought his daughter along.

"Hell yeah. Today is your son birthday, huh?"

"Yeah. He thinks he's grown today," Sammy said.

"I know the feeling. My name is Hiss, by the way."

"I'm Sammy."

"Nice to meet you." Lil Hiss couldn't lie, Sammy was a good looking woman, and he like her attitude and energy.

They talked the whole time at Six Flags, enjoying each other's company, laughing and vibing. Before going different ways, they exchanged numbers.

Driving home, all types of thoughts popped in her head. She felt like Hiss could be that somebody special in her life that she needed.

***

Downtown, Atlanta

Elisa walked into a therapist's office for the first time in her life. She felt like this was really needed because waking up in cold sweats every night was getting old.

"Excuse me, I'm here to see Janice," Elisa said to the lady sitting at the front desk, filing her nails.

"She is in room six down the hall," the clerk said, not even looking at Elisa.

"Ok, thank you," Elisa walked down the hall a little nervous, not really knowing what to expect. She knocked on the door and heard a female voice tell her to come inside.

Walking into the room, it looked like some shit off a movie, when a patient goes to speak to a professional psych.

"You must be Elisa. Please, come in. have a seat," Ms. Janice stated, standing up to greet Elisa.

Elisa was surprised at how pretty Ms. Janice was, and how young she looked.

"You pretty," Elisa said.

"Thanks. You are too," Janice said, pulling out her pen and pad.

"How long have you been doing this? Helping people?" Elisa asked.

"Close to 10 years now," Ms. Janice said.

"Oh wow."

"Let's start with why are you here?" Ms. Janice asked.

"Well, I been having nightmares and cold sweats about my childhood," Elisa said.

"Let's talk about that."

"Where to start?" Elisa asked.

"Childhood, let's start with that," Ms. Janice stated.

"Ok. Well, growing up, I was raped a lot, by different men. I was forced to have sex with grown men at the age of 12, and all the way up into 12th grade in high school." Elisa was trying to hold her real emotions back.

"I'm sorry for what happen, but I see you encountered a lot of hurt and pain." Ms. Janice said.

"I did."

"Talk about it," Ms. Janice stated.

Coke Girlz

"Can we save that for the next session, please" Elisa asked.
"Sure."
"When are you free?" Elisa asked, wanting to come back.
"When do want to come back?" Janice asked.
"In a few days."
"Ok, cool. Just call me so you can set an appointment."
"Thank you," Elisa stated, getting ready to leave.
"Elisa, try not to think about your past," Ms. Janice said.
"I'll try," Elisa said, leaving.

***

West End, Atlanta

Style was in the West End section, hustling with his boy Promo. Ashanti had just dropped off some keys to him this morning, and he couldn't believe what happened.

Ashanti doubled him this time, giving him 10 keys of coke. Style had a nice little piece of change already saved, thanks to his new plug.

"Style," Promo shouted, coming into the playground, where a gang of niggas were hanging out at.

"Aye, shawty."

"I just recruited some little nigga from Niggaville and Cascade," Promo said. Style nodded. He was ready to take over Zone 4.

Chapter 41

Southside, Atlanta

Club Ocean 66 was the hot spot tonight. Big Loot was posted up in a small section, with a few of his hitters, having a good time.

Big Loot was a four-hundred-pound man, with a fake eye and a funny walk, somewhat like a limp.

Getting money was something Big Loot had been doing since his early teens because his dad was a plug in Alabama, which was right next door to the A.

Zone one was his stomping ground, all the way from Hollywood Court PJs to Rachel Walk PJs. Making $20,000 to $50,000 every other day wasn't real money to him, so he'd been expanding to other zones.

There was at least nine dancers in the section with Big Loot, but two of them he was familiar with from other clubs.

"Hey Big Nasty," Cream said, with her sexy voice, sitting in his lap as he sipped on Henny, getting wasted.

"What's your name again, sweetheart?" Big Loot asked.

"Cream, and this my girl, Sayla," Cream said, as Sayla approached them, with her titties hanging out and her G-string stuck in the slit of her bold pussy.

Big Loot was staring at Sayla's sexy body, at a loss for words.

"How much to eat da pretty little cat, shawty?" Big Loot asked Sayla, as Cream grinded on his lap, trying to find his penis and holding back her laugh.

"You ain't got enough paper for this, zaddyyyy." Sayla stunted on him, seeing a sour look appear on his face.

"Bitch, you know who the fuck I am?" Big Loot pulled out wads of money from his pockets.

"Ok, Big Money," Cream said, still dancing to the rap music.

"I want the both of you," Big Loot said, feeling as if Sayla was trying to play him like a broke nigga.

"Ok. What you waiting on?" Cream asked, getting up. She and Sayla walked off to get dressed to leave.

In minutes, Cream and Sayla were outside, looking at Big Loot standing next to a gray Cadillac truck, with big rims and dark tints.

"Drive. I got a condo downtown near the Underground Mall." Big Loot handed Sayla the keys. Walking around the SUV, he climbed into the passenger seat.

"Ok, big boy." Sayla gave Cream a look before Cream got in the backseat.

The drive to his condo was funny to them because Big Loot passed out, and was snoring loud.

Big Loot woke up once they yelled his name, trying to figure out where he lived.

"Where you live?" Sayla asked, driving through the empty downtown streets.

"Double back, you just passed it," Big Loot said, farting.

"Oh shit." Sayla did a quick U-turn, hoping police were nowhere in sight because they had weapons in their purses.

"Right here, this big building. Park across the street and come on." Big Loot was feeling himself, thanks to the Henny he'd been on all night.

The girls followed him into the condo, through the lobby, and took an elevator ride to the suite.

Big Loot let them inside the condo. They liked how the place was decorated. He had taste, but the place had a strong odor to it.

"Nice," Cream said.

"Let's get nasty. I want you to suck my dick, and you eat my ass," Big Loot said with a serious expression. Both women looked at each other as if he was bugging.

Big Loot started to get undressed, and they took charge, pulling out their guns on him. By the time he got done taking off his six X shirt, he saw two pistols pointing at him.

This was his sixth time being robbed in the same year, so he knew what to do and how to save his life, by any means.

"There is a safe under the bed," Big Loot stated.

"Code?" Sayla asked.

"2-44-1-17. Please, just let me slide, shawty." Big Loot's man breasts were bigger than the both of theirs. They were disgusted.

Coke Girlz

    Cream went to the bedroom to check for the safe.
    "Y'all finna do Big Loot like this?"
    "Nigga, shut your freak ass up," Sayla said, getting a text, most likely from Ashanti and Faith. They were outside as their backup.
    Ashanti followed them when they left the club. She needed to keep an eye on them and make sure shit went right. Cream came out from the back with six Louis Vuitton pillowcases full of money and drugs.
    "Damn. He was doing it big," Cream said.
    "We straight?" Big Loot asked, hoping they'd just leave.
    Bloc. Bloc. Bloc. Bloc. Bloc. Bloc. Bloc. Bloc.
    Sayla shot Big Loot in his chest, killing him instantly, before they left. Outside, Ashanti was in a Yukon truck, awaiting them as they got in with the shit from the lick. Happy and turned up, they were about to be up. Cream knew this was her breakthrough to quit dancing. She was on now.

Coke Girlz

Chapter 42

College Park, Georgia

Ashanti drove the girls to a local park in her old hood, where she grew up.

"What y'all finna do with y'all cut?" Ashanti asked, pulling over in a small parking lot area.

"Buy me a new car, gurl," Sayla said.

"I'ma open me up a small business because I'm sick of dancing," Cream said, wondering where they were.

"My cousin crib over there. We gonna split everything inside," Faith said, getting out, as the girls all climbed out. Cream and Sayla grabbed the bags out the back.

When Sayla and Cream grabbed the bags out the back, Ashanti and Faith stood there with guns pointed at their heads.

Sayla and Cream's smiles both quickly faded.

"Sorry, girls, but I think the fun ends here," Faith stated, snatching the pillowcases from both women.

"You grimy bitch," Cream said, feeling the double cross.

"I consider myself a grimy diva," Ashanti said before pulling the trigger on both women. Their bodies collapsed into the SUV doors, slowly hitting the ground.

A white Benz pulled up right on time. It was Eddy, driving Ashanti's car.

"Y'all some crazy bitches. Come on before the boys come," Eddy said as Ashanti and Faith got in with pillow cases.

"Thanks for coming, baby," Ashanti said, giving her man a kiss on the lips.

"So this is the handsome man you been talking about?" Faith asked, seeing how sexy Ed was again, for the second time.

"Yeah. Don't look too hard," Ashanti joked, but she really meant it.

"Where we going?" Ed added.

"To Faith's crib," Ashanti told him.

"Ight. Where is that at?" Ed drove through the dark Atlanta streets with guns, money, and work in a 150,000 dollar car.

He knew this wasn't a bright idea, so when they got to their location, he planned to tell Ashanti about herself.

Ashanti and Ed had both been talking about moving into a house together, since they were really taking each other serious.

It was really his idea for her to cut the strippers off because they could end up being a potential hole in what she was trying to build.

He told her selling drugs was a very different game from robbing. But she told him whatever happens, she was willing to deal with it, good and bad.

Eddy had never met a gangster bitch like Ashanti. He really felt she was the one for him.

"What's his cut?" Faith said, referring to Ed. She was looking into the pillowcases full of money and keys.

"He don't want shit. My baby getting to a bag," Ashanti added.

"I could use some gas money for the gas I put in your empty gas tank. Y'all got me out here at all hours of the night."

"Don't worry, I'll make up for it, baby," Ashanti said, rubbing his legs and licking her lips, letting him know it was going down when they got home.

"Y'all nasty." Faith caught their little eye contact.

Faith was glad Ashanti had finally found a real man that made her smile. It made her want to find real love. She always got unlucky in that field, so she stayed away until Mr. Right found her.

***

Union City Jail

Jason had a visit that a correction officer had told him about a few minutes ago. He was hoping this was a visit from his lawyer, so he can find out what was really about to happen. With four murders, he knew his life would be done.

He'd been stressing hard. He'd gotten his first call the other day, and called a chick he was cool with because he kept a large sum of money at her home.

Coke Girlz

His second call was to his mom, Megan, who basically cried the whole call and told him he should've listened to her a long time ago.

On the visit, he saw Ashanti sitting there with a sad face. He knew he'd let her down. She used to look up to him.

"Oh my god, I just saw you on the news yesterday. Then Candra texted me this morning. What's going to happen?" She was nervous and scared for him.

"Relax, sis. I'ma get two lawyers. I have one already paid for, but I want you to focus on these two things I'm about to tell you," he said, having her full attention.

"Anything," she shot back.

"One of the main rats is Alex," he told her, looking at her shocked facial expression.

"My ex, Alex?"

"Yeah. I saw the statements. And I think there's another man that goes by the name Lil Hiss," he said.

"What you need me to do?"

"You're very smart, Ashanti. But also, I'ma call you later so you can go get some shit from my crib before the feds hit that one, too."

"Ok. I know what to do." Ashanti had tears in her eyes.

"Don't cry. Where there's a will, there's a way. Love you, sis. Be safe. You're a gangsta bitch at heart."

Chapter 43

Zoo of Atlanta

Candra and her boyfriend, Isaac, were out on a date. She couldn't believe he took her to the zoo, but Candra was really having a great time.

"You really brought me to a zoo?" she asked, holding his hand.

"Something new. Plus, you can learn some things about a few wild animals," Isaac told her, looking at a gorilla walk back and forth on his knuckles, in a small cage, inside of a cave.

"I'm learning every day," she joked.

"You got jokes, huh, big head?" Isaac tapped her nose.

They spent a lot of time together. When she was in class or studying was the only time they separated.

Since they'd met at a party, they'd been stuck to each other like glue. He loved everything about her.

Isaac was a brother of four, raised in a section called West End, which had a large population of Muslims. Isaac's whole family was Muslim, including himself.

Out of all of his brothers, he was the only one who loved a regular lifestyle, working as a manager for an Amazon warehouse.

Candra told him about her brother being arrested for a few murders. When she brought it to his attention, he remembered seeing the case on the news a while back.

He'd been comforting her since the news because her brother had been the only male figure in their life, since they were kids. Candra didn't know her father, and she didn't even care for meeting him, if he was even alive.

They went out to eat at Red Lobster before she had to get back to class.

***

Zone 1, Atlanta

Eddy and Ashanti had just come from meeting Buzz, dropping his part of the cut she got from her last robbery.

"Do you really think this shit you doing going to last forever?" Ed asked her.

"Shit, do you? Because you basically do the same thing as me," she caught an attitude. Ashanti was on her period, so she was moody.

Ed didn't really know how crazy Ashanti got at that time of the month.

"You on some bullshit, I see, Ashanti."

"No. You just say dumb shit."

"Did you see your uncle's eyes when you gave him the drugs? I thought he was about to rob you," Ed said, trying to get a laugh out of her. But she wasn't joking.

"I did." Ashanti's reply was short and flat.

Eddy knew she was upset about her brother being locked up. Ed knew Jason was in a shit load of trouble. He hoped he wasn't in none of Jason's cases because they'd put in a lot of work together.

"I'ma take you home. I have to go handle some business," Ed said, starting to get frustrated with her.

"Good." she crossed her arms, not feeling his energy now.

"Fine," he shot back, stopping at a red light.

"Look out, Ed," she yelled, seeing two men on motorcycles coming towards them, with sub machine guns.

Tat. Tat. Tat. Tat. Tat. Tat. Tat. Tat. Tat.

Bullets hit the Benz, but Ed hit the gas, racing off. He knew if he didn't, they would be dead. The shooters on the bikes didn't even bother to follow them because a police station was a few blocks away.

"You good?" Ed asked Ashanti.

"Yes. That was close. Who the fuck was that?" Ashanti's heart was still racing. She'd never been shot and she didn't have it nowhere in her plans to get hit.

"I don't know who it was, but I'ma find out who put all these holes in my car." Ed had so many ops, he couldn't just point out one person.

Coke Girlz

"I'm wit you."

"No, you're not. Your ass going home, like I told you," he said sternly.

"Damn. Whatever," she loved to be controlled, at times, and Ed was turning her on right now.

***

B-Ham, Alabama

Faith had a lot of family in Alabama, in a city called Birmingham, aka Magic City. She used to go out there a lot as a kid. She used to love it. She went out to a family reunion, looking good, dripping in Chanel, with her hair and nails done.

The park was full of family members she didn't even know, but most she did. This was her father's side of the family.

"Faith," two young men yelled, leaning on Impalas, which were sitting on big rims with crazy paint jobs. Their cars caught everybody's attention.

"Mask and Blast, what's up?" she said, approaching her cousins.

"That was your BMW?" Blast asked, looking at her jewelry, wondering if her ice was real.

"Yeah," Faith replied.

"We ain't see you in a while. It looks like you doing ok for yourself in Atlanta," Mask, who was the cuter one, stated.

Growing up, she and Mask did some fondling when they were kids, but they didn't really understand how they were related.

"I'm doing me. But I see y'all not too far behind," she said.

"We run the shit out here, thanks to your Uncle Jim and your brother, Mike," Blast added.

"Step brother," she corrected them. Her and her step brother never saw eye to eye.

"He just copped a Wraith and a Bentley truck. I'm next up," Blast said, speaking about her step brother.

"Good for him. I'ma go see grandmom and chill. See y'all," Faith said, walking off, as they looked at her ass wobble in her outfit.

Coke Girlz

Chapter 44

Macon, GA
Weeks later

The nice mini mansion in a quiet neighborhood belonged to a drug dealer by the name of Lil Hiss. He loved the quiet neighborhood on the outskirts of the city.

The five bedroom, three bathroom home with two walk in closets, a stocked bar, and exercise room, had a four car garage, where he kept his favorite cars.

Lil Hiss had a nice set up for dinner with his guest, Sammy. It had been four weeks since they'd first met and he was really into her feeling her vibes.

Sammy was different, that's what he liked about her. She was smart, calm, sexy, classy, and a diva, all in one. He ordered some catered food from an expensive, black owned restaurant in Atlanta. Lil Hiss had been so busy with his kids that he had no time for a woman. Having Sammy around tonight was what he really needed right now.

Lil Hiss sent two of his men at Ed, but they missed. He knew next time his goons wouldn't miss their chance.

Now Jason was gone, locked up for four murders. He knew Ed was Jason's right hand man, or at least in the same circle. Word on the street was that Eddy was nothing to fuck with, so he wanted to get him out the way before he became a victim.

Lil Hiss had family, workers, and shooters all through Atlanta, so finding Ed wouldn't be too hard.

As he was setting up a few candles to give the dining room that good mood, he heard the doorbell ring.

"Time to party," he said out loud, going for the front door.

Opening the door, he saw Sammy standing there in a nice, black, designer dress, with heels. Sammy's hair was in a neat little bun, showing her beautiful facial features.

"You look sexy."

"Thanks. Nice house," Sammy said, walking inside, admiring his taste.

"Thanks. I got everything set up in the dining room. I hope you hungry," he said, looking at her phat ass, knowing she was gonna have some good pussy because of the way she walked.

"What's on the menu?" Sammy asked, looking at all the food on the table.

"Everything."

"I don't eat meat."

"Ok. I have vegan meals to your left," he said, as she finally sat her purse down on the table.

"How about you come and feed me some fruit," Sammy said, reaching for a bowl of grapes.

"I got you. Let me go wash my hands." Lil Hiss ran into the kitchen to wash his hands, trying to calm himself down because his dick was poking out in his pants.

Walking back into the dining room area, he had to make sure he wasn't tripping when he saw Sammy standing up pointing a handgun at him.

"Sit he fuck down, now," she yelled, with her serious face.

"Calm down. Don't shoot." Lil Hiss was hoping to talk her down.

Bloc.

She fired a shot into the wall above his head, almost killing him.

"Hoe nigga, sit down," Sammy's voice was harder. He did what he was told to do now.

"What do you want?"

"Everything you have," Sammy replied, with no shame.

"In my garage, as soon as you walk in, look into the ceiling and push it open. There you will see two trash bags and a black suitcase. That's everything I have. I swear, on everything." Lil Hiss' voice got a little raspy, as if he wanted to cry.

"You lying to me?"

"No. I swear on my mama, mama," Lil Hiss was about to beg.

Bloc.

Bloc.

Coke Girlz

Bloc.
Bloc.
Bloc.
Bullets hit Lil Hiss in the head, and the rest hit his neck, killing him.

She stood there, watching his soul leave his frail body. Sammy walked around the table to grab some more grapes because she was really hungry.

The garage had a door that was connected to the kitchen, and she easily found it. Walking into the garage, she realized she needed a boost to reach the ceiling. She saw a stepper and started pushing up the ceiling, trying to find his belongings. Within seconds, she did.

She found everything he said, two bags of money, filled with all types of bills, and a suitcase with 22 keys of dope.

Sammy left the crib and called her bestie, Ashanti, to tell her what she came up on by herself. Sammy had a feeling Lil Hiss was a baller from his conversations on the phone, so she had it set in her head he would be her first practice victim. But she had no clue he was holding like this.

Romell Tukes

Coke Girlz

Chapter 45

4th Ward, Atlanta

Ashanti parked in the Holiday Inn parking lot and waited on Sammy to arrive to see what was going on. Sammy called while Ashanti and Ed were in the middle of a makeup sex session.

Sammy sounded like it was some type of emergency, so she rushed out of her crib, looking like anything.

Things had been going so good, she couldn't believe it. Style was bringing in so much money daily that she knew that a plug was well needed. She didn't want to buy drugs from Buzz, so she asked Ed to look around and plug shop for her. He was more than willing.

She saw Sammy's car speed into the hotel parking lot, flying over speed bumps, as if they weren't there.

Ashanti grabbed her purse, with her gun in it, and got out of the car, hoping she was ok.

Sammy jumped out with the biggest smile she'd ever seen.

"I did it, girl." Sammy approached Ashanti with a warm hug.

"What the fuck is going on?" Ashanti pulled back from the hug, smelling gunpowder on Sammy's body.

"Let me tell the story from the start. I met a man at Six Flags for my son's birthday party, and we just started vibing and kicking it." Sammy paused, looking around the lot nervously.

"I know you ain't call me out cha to talk about some nigga." Ashanti was about to get pissed.

"Let me finished bitch, damn. So I knew he was getting some big money from his elegant style and our talks. I came up with a quick plan to make my move, and it worked." Sammy was cheerful.

"So what happened?"

"I robbed the nigga and I killed him," Sammy said with excitement.

"Bitch, you lying." Ashanti couldn't believe her girl went ham already.

"Oh yeah, peep this shit." Sammy popped the trunk.

189

Ashanti saw the bags of money, and drugs in a suitcase Sammy popped open.

"Damn, you did it, for real." Ashanti couldn't believe it.

"The drugs are for you. I know you know what to do with them better than me," Sammy said.

"You sure? You can make some real money off all this shit," Ashanti told her.

"Nah, that's for you. We partners now. Big facts," Sammy stated.

"Ok, but I'ma give you half of the earnings," Ashanti told her.

"I'll take that."

"Who was the dude?'

"Some cat named Hiss," Sammy stated, as Ashanti's eyes widened.

"Hold on. Lil Hiss?" Ashanti had to make sure she was hearing this correctly. This could be the same man she'd been looking for, but he'd been hard to find.

"Yes. He told me that was his younger name," Sammy stated.

"I can't believe this."

"Why? What's wrong?" Sammy hoped the man she killed wasn't related to Ashanti because her reaction to the robbery was awkward.

"Nothing. It's cool. You did a good job, too good," Ashanti said, taking the suitcase.

"I am going to get a new car, buy my son some shit, and live for a few days. I'ma call you," Sammy said, closing the trunk.

"Ok. Be safe," Ashanti said. Then she saw Alex's car parked in the cut to her left, as Sammy got in her car to leave.

Ashanti couldn't believe Alex put his hands on her and snitched on her brother. She hadn't seen him or heard from him since that day he hit her.

She waited in the car for him to come out. Thirty minutes later, he came out in a wheelchair, being pushed by a pretty chick.

Ashanti wasted no time in hopping out like a madwoman and blicking off shots.

Boc.

Coke Girlz

Boc.
Boc.
Boc.
Ashanti killed Alex and the woman he was with, who was pushing his wheelchair.

"Rat ass nigga," she said, getting back in her car and racing off.

***

Zone 1 Precinct, Atlanta

Buzz was in the police station, sweating bullets. He'd just been caught with two hundred and twenty keys of coke in his house, in a drug raid.

He'd been in a cold room with double glass mirrors for three hours, scared to death. Officer Mike and Detective Halls were both on the other side of the glass, watching his every move, laughing.

Buzz felt crazy. He'd let two dirty cops put him in the trick bag because he knew someone was watching him the whole time, but he didn't want to overlook something.

Twenty-five keys were found in his garage, which was supposed to be for Ed and two workers in East Atlanta.

Detective Halls walked in with her badge hanging from her chest.

"OG Buzz, good to have you," she said, sitting down across from Buzz, opening up a folder, and humming a song.

"Do we have to go through all of this?" Buzz asked.

"I hope no. You know what needs to be done. This ain't your first time in this situation," Detective Halls said, knowing Buzz's background real well.

A long time ago, Buzz had gotten caught with forty-six keys of dope. To get out of his jam, he ratted on two big plugs, which led to a 62 man federal indictment.

"There is a man named Mills, from Zone One, and a Muslim cat named Heat getting some big money all throughout the state."

"We know Mills, but Heat we're not so familiar with," Detective Halls said.

"Heat supplies Mills, but he live in another state. He's big time, but I believe he works for someone bigger." Buzz had no remorse for snitching.

"Give me everything you know, and it better be all right," Detective Halls said, as she went in.

Coke Girlz

Chapter 46

Atlanta, GA

Ed took Ashanti to a well-known sneaker spot, called Georgia 400 Shoe Outlet, in the city. He hadn't taken her out there so she could shop. He'd come out to meet the biggest plug in the city.

"You sure he gonna buy it because everybody know your field of work, baby," she told him.

"Me and dude go way back. Trust me, he know what's up," Ed stated, parking.

"Ight. I have all the money in the trunk."

"We might not even need that, shawty. But I'll be back in ten minutes," Ed said, seeing a yellow Rolls Royce, looking clean.

Ed knew how important it was for Ashanti to get a plug so she could get real money. Ed could have taken over the drug game a long time ago, but that life wasn't for him. Plus, he loved his life.

The man climbed out of the driver's seat of the Ghost, happy to see his childhood friend, Eddy. He was the one who'd given him the nickname "Ed."

"Damn, boy, you looking good," Ed said.

"Same to you. I been hearing good things about you since I have been back in the city," Heat stated, leaning against his car.

"I been doing me, bruh." Ed took off his hat. It was a hot day outside.

"I been in Miami, doing big things, but I've been a little back and forth, handling my one, two." Heat told him.

Eddy and Heat grew up together. They were close, and both cut from the same cloth. Heat had three brothers that Eddy knew of; Isaac, Greg, and the young brother they called Young Ock.

Heat's whole family were Muslims, and devoted to their clean.

"I need to speak to you about some money issues, bruh, I need a plug." Ed cut straight to the point.

"You sell drugs now?" Heat laughed. He never thought he would see this day because Ed was a born killer.

"It's for my girlfriend. She official, bro. Facts." Ed stamped her so Heat knew it was official.

"Ight. I'ma do it for you, bro. But I only deal with you," Heat said.

"Deal."

"Ight. Call me in two days," Heat said, leaving.

When Ed got back to the car, Ashanti was looking odd.

"How did it go?'

"Good. It's a deal. But he only wants to deal with me," he said.

"Ok, cool, but what's his name anyway?" she asked, knowing the man looked very familiar. But he had his back to her.

"Heat."

"Heat, oh." Ashanti now remembered she'd met Heat in Miami, at a club.

"He really run the city, but he be low key."

"Good."

"We about to be rich, now," Ed said.

"I know. Can't wait," Ashanti said, but her mind was elsewhere, watching the Ghost leave the lot.

***

Zone One, Atlanta

Mills made plans to go to North Carolina for the weekend, so he left all the money and drugs with his brother, Lil Mills.

He trusted his little brother to run the show while he was gone, hands down, but he'd been seeing a lot of weird shit the past two weeks.

Cars had been tailing him. His cell phone had been acting up, so he felt like it was time to get out of town for a while.

He was in his son's room, at his baby's mother's crib, who he didn't fuck with at all. She was a dirt bag and shiesty person. She had two other kids by his cousins.

"Soon."

"When is soon, dad?" Lil Rakeem asked, holding his favorite teddy bear.

Coke Girlz

"Before Christmas, I promise."

"You promise?" Lil Rakeem didn't want his dad to go because they did everything together.

"Yes, I promise. Now go to sleep, big head." Mills kissed his son on the forehead before turning off the lights in his room.

Mills walked downstairs to see his baby's mother sitting on the couch in sexy lingerie, crossing her thick legs, drinking wine, and staring at him.

"I left a bag of money in the closet for him. It's $200,000. That should hold him down," Mills said, walking past her.

"Wait, damn. Come sit down real quick. I don't bite unless you let me," Erica said, licking her phat lips. Her head game was crazy, but he wasn't trying to downgrade anymore.

"I'm good."

"Fuck you, deadbeat ass nigga," she shouted out loud.

Mills laughed, walking outside to his Bentley coupe.

"Freeze." Ten cops jumped out from the backyard, out of cars, and black vans pulled up with federal agents. Mills dropped to the ground and got cuffed up. He was being held on a 22 men fed indictment.

Romell Tukes

Chapter 47

Zone 4, Atlanta

Young Ock and his cousin, Gram, rode around in Young Ock's blacked out Hellcat, with tints. They listened to a Young Thug mixtape, one of Young Ock's favorite rappers.

"When you heard about these new little niggas trying to take over Zone 4?" Young Ock asked, fresh from his LA trip.

"These little niggas been out here for a few weeks now," Gram stated.

"Why I am just hearing about these dudes, bruh? Come on, cuz, you supposed to be out here holding dis shit down," Young Ock told his older cousin Gram, who ran a few of his traps for him.

Young Ock was a twenty-one year old hustler. He was about his paper, but he also played with that pistol when it was time for smoke. His other three brothers played a big part in his life, especially Heat, who was his drug connect.

Being from Zone 4, he felt as if he owned the section of the city. There were a few other drug dealers around, but none of them could add up to Young Ock and his crew.

When he got back from his trip to LA, he started hearing rumors about a new clique in the city, trying to take over. One thing Young Ock refused to let happen was for some no name niggas to take over his hood.

"I tried to call, bruh, but your shit was going to voicemail," Gram stated, looking at niggas hustle in the Oakland City hood he was from.

Gram was thirty years old and a big time dope boy, but he was a calm cat, not really one for violence or dumb shit. He preferred to get money and stay out the way.

"I got two phones my, nigga."

"I ain't got your other number, dawgy," Gram shot back, not in the mood to argue because he'd been going at it with his baby's mother all morning.

"What do you even know about these cats, dawg?" Young Ock wanted to find out who and what he was about to be up against.

"All I know is the main nigga is named Style," Gram protested.

"Style? Didn't he kill Shawty G from College Park?"

"I don't know, bro."

"He used to run with Top Shot and the nigga Real, who both got bodied recently." Young Ock knew Real well, so he'd heard about the two wild young niggas.

"I think I know shawty now. I'm thinking he a hothead, but word is he moving a lot of weight," Gram stated, thinking of Real and Top Shot.

"Out da blue, huh?" Young Ock knew there was something wrong with that.

"I believe so."

"Look more into the shit," Young Ock told his cousin.

"Got cha, bruh."

Young Ock dropped Gram off at his crib, thinking about this Style nigga, who was now on his radar.

***

B-ham, Atlanta

Faith had just gotten the news her uncle was killed last night, and her stepbrother was shot up, leaving him unstable in a coma. They got shot up outside of a club in Fairfield, where four other people got shot, also.

Faith and her uncle were best friends when he was living in Atlanta, before he moved back to Alabama. He'd helped raise her.

A few nights ago, they were all having a good time at the uncle's mansion, smoking and drinking. Her uncle pulled her aside and told her, if anything ever happened to him, he would not want her to cry. Then he gave her a piece of paper with an address on it that read "only if I'm dead."

Today she was on her way to that address, using her cousin's car. Faith was going back to Atlanta next week, until this happened.

Coke Girlz

She told Ashanti and Elisa they would have to do without her for a while.

She did miss her girls and family, but she had family out here, too, that needed her right now.

On Sunday morning, most people were at church or sleep, but not in the Woodlawn area. People were outside all over the place this morning.

Faith saw the small brick building with the house number 192 on the side, which was the same address on the paper her uncle gave her.

After parking, she was nervous. *Why would he even want me to come here?* She thought to herself, walking up the cement stairs.

The front door was unlocked, so she walked in. The crib was basically empty, with a couch and a few normal items laying around.

"What I am looking for?" She asked herself, walking around looking in closets and cabinets.

Faith went to the back room, searching with no clue to what she was looking for, until she sat down.

"What the fuck?" Faith said, sitting down and feeling something funny under her. Faith got up and pulled back the satin sheets. She saw a zipper in the middle of the bed. Pulling down the long zipper, she almost fainted when she saw all the keys and money stacked up neatly.

"Oh my God," she screamed, thinking there had to be at least two million dollars and over five hundred bricks. Tears formed in her eyes. She knew it was time to finish what her uncle started.

***

Union City Federal Jail
Two Months Later

Mills was sick in his jail cell, thinking about how this shit just went down.

He was the leader of his indictment, and the charges were ranging from murders to drug trafficking.

"Mr. Patterson, you have a visit, and you have five minutes to get ready," a C.O. said, coming to his cell.

"Ight. Get the fuck away from my door," Mills said, getting off the bed.

Mills heard Jason was on the other side of the jail. He couldn't wait to see him so he could knock him out.

In Mills' paperwork, the FBI said Mills' crew was into a serious beef with Jason and his crew in Stone Mountain.

Durk and Lil Hiss were also on the indictment, and said to have orchestrated a few murders and attempts.

Mills also had been hearing there was a group of women going around robbing niggas for money and drugs. Mills knew there was something going on when DJ, Woop, Coral, Big Loot, and Kay all popped up dead.

Women were connected to all the crimes, and he found it odd, even though a nigga could've set it up. But what if a group of bitches were really out killing shit.

Mills didn't want to over think it, but he felt something was missing.

He went to his visit, already knowing it was his little brother, who'd been holding shit down for him.

***

Lil Mills waited for his big brother to come down, but he was taking forever.

Coming to jail visits was something he hated, especially a federal hold over jail, because his name was in the system. There was a lot of inmates' girlfriends eyeing him, but he paid them no mind. He didn't want to knock a nigga out.

Lil Mills was twenty and a pro boxer, one of the best in Atlanta, but he had a second job, hustling. Since his brother had been locked up, he'd been running the show for him.

Mills walked out with his bop and tough guy look.

Coke Girlz

"What's up, bruh? Thanks for coming out," Mills said.

"Of course. How you been? Did the lawyer come through?" Lil Mills asked.

"I saw the lawyer. We filing some motions, but I need you to handle the main source of this," Mills stated, giving his brother the eye.

"Like a rat?"

"Damn, nigga, you act like you slow and can't read between the fucking lines." Mills got upset because he was frustrated with everything.

"Ight, cuz. Who?"

"Buzz. He an old head, getting to a bag. He be all over, so be on point."

"I got it. But I got a new chick I been seeing. She fire too, cuz," Lil Mills said because Mills disliked his last one.

"Ok. What's her name? And watch them bitches out there."

"Her name Elisa. Shawty bad, with her own bag," Lil Mills smiled, thinking about his new wifey he'd been seeing.

"Glad you happy. But I need you to really focus on this money," Mills said.

"Of course. I'm on it," Lil Mills said. They spent the rest of the visit talking about Jason, Money, Buzz, and family.

***

Zone 6, Atlanta

Ashanti was on facetime with Jason for the first time. She was on her way to pick up Ed, but she had to pull over because today Jason would sign a plea agreement.

"Hey, bro. you got big as hell. I'm coming to see you tomorrow," she said, seeing he looked good.

"I just copped out to sixty-five years, Ashanti."

"What?" she shouted, as tears quickly flooded her eyes.

"It's cool, don't stress. I can get an appeal. But I saw all the paperwork and statements today. And guess who, besides Alex, was about to take the stand on me and tried to end my fucking life?" he asked.

"Who?"

"If I tell you, Ashanti, you know what I need you to do, right?" Jason asked.

"Yes, and I will. Who?" she repeated

Before he could say a name, the facetime call disconnected.

"Jason. Jason. Jason." Ashanti was pissed. The call was done and her blood was boiling. Ashanti knew someone was about to pay for this shit they did to her brother.

To Be Continued…
Coke Girlz 2
Coming Soon

Coke Girlz

Lock Down Publications and Ca$h Presents assisted publishing packages.

BASIC PACKAGE $499

Editing

Cover Design

Formatting

UPGRADED PACKAGE $800

Typing

Editing

Cover Design

Formatting

ADVANCE PACKAGE $1,200

Typing

Editing

Cover Design

Formatting

Copyright registration

Proofreading

Upload book to Amazon

Romell Tukes

LDP SUPREME PACKAGE $1,500

Typing

Editing

Cover Design

Formatting

Copyright registration

Proofreading

Set up Amazon account

Upload book to Amazon

Advertise on LDP Amazon and Facebook page

***Other services available upon request. Additional charges may apply

Lock Down Publications

P.O. Box 944

Stockbridge, GA 30281-9998

Phone # 470 303-9761

Coke Girlz

Submission Guideline

Submit the first three chapters of your completed manuscript to ldpsubmissions@gmail.com, subject line: Your book's title. The manuscript must be in a .doc file and sent as an attachment. Document should be in Times New Roman, double spaced and in size 12 font. Also, provide your synopsis and full contact information. If sending multiple submissions, they must each be in a separate email.

Have a story but no way to send it electronically? You can still submit to LDP/Ca$h Presents. Send in the first three chapters, written or typed, of your completed manuscript to:

LDP: Submissions Dept
Po Box 944
Stockbridge, Ga 30281

DO NOT send original manuscript. Must be a duplicate.

Provide your synopsis and a cover letter containing your full contact information.

Thanks for considering LDP and Ca$h Presents.

NEW RELEASES

BETRAYAL OF A THUG by FRE$H
THE STREETS WILL TALK by YOLANDA MOORE
THE COCAINE PRINCESS by KING RIO
THE BILLIONAIRE BENTLEYS by VON DIESEL
COKE GIRLZ by ROMELL TUKES

Coke Girlz

Coming Soon from Lock Down Publications/Ca$h Presents
BLOOD OF A BOSS **VI**
SHADOWS OF THE GAME II
TRAP BASTARD II
By **Askari**
LOYAL TO THE GAME **IV**
By **T.J. & Jelissa**
IF TRUE SAVAGE **VIII**
MIDNIGHT CARTEL IV
DOPE BOY MAGIC IV
CITY OF KINGZ III
NIGHTMARE ON SILENT AVE II
THE PLUG OF LIL MEXICO II
By **Chris Green**
BLAST FOR ME **III**
A SAVAGE DOPEBOY III
CUTTHROAT MAFIA III
DUFFLE BAG CARTEL VII
HEARTLESS GOON VI
By **Ghost**
A HUSTLER'S DECEIT III
KILL ZONE II
BAE BELONGS TO ME III
By **Aryanna**
KING OF THE TRAP III
By **T.J. Edwards**
GORILLAZ IN THE BAY V
3X KRAZY III
STRAIGHT BEAST MODE II
De'Kari

Romell Tukes

KINGPIN KILLAZ IV
STREET KINGS III
PAID IN BLOOD III
CARTEL KILLAZ IV
DOPE GODS III
Hood Rich
SINS OF A HUSTLA II
ASAD
RICH $AVAGE II
By Martell Troublesome Bolden
YAYO V
Bred In The Game 2
S. Allen
CREAM III
THE STREETS WILL TALK II
By Yolanda Moore
SON OF A DOPE FIEND III
HEAVEN GOT A GHETTO II
By Renta
LOYALTY AIN'T PROMISED III
By Keith Williams
I'M NOTHING WITHOUT HIS LOVE II
SINS OF A THUG II
TO THE THUG I LOVED BEFORE II
IN A HUSTLER I TRUST II
By Monet Dragun
QUIET MONEY IV
EXTENDED CLIP III
THUG LIFE IV
By **Trai'Quan**

Coke Girlz

THE STREETS MADE ME IV
By **Larry D. Wright**
IF YOU CROSS ME ONCE II
By **Anthony Fields**
THE STREETS WILL NEVER CLOSE III
By K'ajji
HARD AND RUTHLESS III
KILLA KOUNTY III
By Khufu
MONEY GAME III
By Smoove Dolla
JACK BOYS VS DOPE BOYS II
A GANGSTA'S QUR'AN V
COKE GIRLZ II
By Romell Tukes
MURDA WAS THE CASE II
Elijah R. Freeman
THE STREETS NEVER LET GO II
By Robert Baptiste
AN UNFORESEEN LOVE III
By **Meesha**
KING OF THE TRENCHES III
by **GHOST & TRANAY ADAMS**

MONEY MAFIA II
LOYAL TO THE SOIL III
By **Jibril Williams**
QUEEN OF THE ZOO II
By **Black Migo**
THE BRICK MAN IV

Romell Tukes

THE COCAINE PRINCESS IV
By King Rio
VICIOUS LOYALTY II
By Kingpen
A GANGSTA'S PAIN II
By J-Blunt
CONFESSIONS OF A JACKBOY III
By Nicholas Lock
GRIMEY WAYS II
By Ray Vinci
KING KILLA II
By Vincent "Vitto" Holloway
BETRAYAL OF A THUG II
By Fre$h

<u>Available Now</u>

RESTRAINING ORDER **I & II**
By **CA$H & Coffee**
LOVE KNOWS NO BOUNDARIES **I II & III**
By **Coffee**
RAISED AS A GOON I, II, III & IV
BRED BY THE SLUMS I, II, III
BLAST FOR ME I & II

Coke Girlz

ROTTEN TO THE CORE I II III
A BRONX TALE I, II, III
DUFFLE BAG CARTEL I II III IV V VI
HEARTLESS GOON I II III IV V
A SAVAGE DOPEBOY I II
DRUG LORDS I II III
CUTTHROAT MAFIA I II
KING OF THE TRENCHES
By **Ghost**
LAY IT DOWN **I & II**
LAST OF A DYING BREED I II
BLOOD STAINS OF A SHOTTA I & II III
By **Jamaica**
LOYAL TO THE GAME I II III
LIFE OF SIN I, II III
By **TJ & Jelissa**
BLOODY COMMAS I & II
SKI MASK CARTEL I II & III
KING OF NEW YORK I II,III IV V
RISE TO POWER I II III
COKE KINGS I II III IV V
BORN HEARTLESS I II III IV
KING OF THE TRAP I II
By **T.J. Edwards**
IF LOVING HIM IS WRONG…I & II
LOVE ME EVEN WHEN IT HURTS I II III
By **Jelissa**
WHEN THE STREETS CLAP BACK I & II III
THE HEART OF A SAVAGE I II III
MONEY MAFIA

Romell Tukes

LOYAL TO THE SOIL I II
By **Jibril Williams**
A DISTINGUISHED THUG STOLE MY HEART I II & III
LOVE SHOULDN'T HURT I II III IV
RENEGADE BOYS I II III IV
PAID IN KARMA I II III
SAVAGE STORMS I II III
AN UNFORESEEN LOVE I II
By **Meesha**
A GANGSTER'S CODE I &, II III
A GANGSTER'S SYN I II III
THE SAVAGE LIFE I II III
CHAINED TO THE STREETS I II III
BLOOD ON THE MONEY I II III
A GANGSTA'S PAIN
By **J-Blunt**
PUSH IT TO THE LIMIT
By **Bre' Hayes**
BLOOD OF A BOSS **I, II, III, IV, V**
SHADOWS OF THE GAME
TRAP BASTARD
By **Askari**
THE STREETS BLEED MURDER **I, II & III**
THE HEART OF A GANGSTA I II& III
By **Jerry Jackson**
CUM FOR ME I II III IV V VI VII VIII
An **LDP Erotica Collaboration**
BRIDE OF A HUSTLA **I II & II**
THE FETTI GIRLS **I, II& III**
CORRUPTED BY A GANGSTA I, II III, IV

Coke Girlz

BLINDED BY HIS LOVE
THE PRICE YOU PAY FOR LOVE I, II ,III
DOPE GIRL MAGIC I II III
By **Destiny Skai**
WHEN A GOOD GIRL GOES BAD
By **Adrienne**
THE COST OF LOYALTY I II III
By Kweli
A GANGSTER'S REVENGE **I II III & IV**
THE BOSS MAN'S DAUGHTERS I II III IV V
A SAVAGE LOVE **I & II**
BAE BELONGS TO ME I II
A HUSTLER'S DECEIT I, II, III
WHAT BAD BITCHES DO I, II, III
SOUL OF A MONSTER I II III
KILL ZONE
A DOPE BOY'S QUEEN I II III
By **Aryanna**
A KINGPIN'S AMBITON
A KINGPIN'S AMBITION **II**
I MURDER FOR THE DOUGH
By **Ambitious**
TRUE SAVAGE I II III IV V VI VII
DOPE BOY MAGIC I, II, III
MIDNIGHT CARTEL I II III
CITY OF KINGZ I II
NIGHTMARE ON SILENT AVE
THE PLUG OF LIL MEXICO II

By **Chris Green**

Romell Tukes

A DOPEBOY'S PRAYER
By **Eddie "Wolf" Lee**
THE KING CARTEL **I, II & III**
By **Frank Gresham**
THESE NIGGAS AIN'T LOYAL **I, II & III**
By **Nikki Tee**
GANGSTA SHYT **I II &III**
By **CATO**
THE ULTIMATE BETRAYAL
By **Phoenix**
BOSS'N UP **I , II & III**
By **Royal Nicole**
I LOVE YOU TO DEATH
By **Destiny J**
I RIDE FOR MY HITTA
I STILL RIDE FOR MY HITTA
By **Misty Holt**
LOVE & CHASIN' PAPER
By **Qay Crockett**
TO DIE IN VAIN
SINS OF A HUSTLA
By **ASAD**
BROOKLYN HUSTLAZ
By **Boogsy Morina**
BROOKLYN ON LOCK I & II
By **Sonovia**
GANGSTA CITY
By **Teddy Duke**
A DRUG KING AND HIS DIAMOND I & II III
A DOPEMAN'S RICHES

Coke Girlz

HER MAN, MINE'S TOO I, II
CASH MONEY HO'S
THE WIFEY I USED TO BE I II
By Nicole Goosby
TRAPHOUSE KING **I II & III**
KINGPIN KILLAZ I II III
STREET KINGS I II
PAID IN BLOOD **I II**
CARTEL KILLAZ I II III
DOPE GODS I II
By **Hood Rich**
LIPSTICK KILLAH **I, II, III**
CRIME OF PASSION I II & III
FRIEND OR FOE I II III
By **Mimi**
STEADY MOBBN' **I, II, III**
THE STREETS STAINED MY SOUL I II III
By **Marcellus Allen**
WHO SHOT YA **I, II, III**
SON OF A DOPE FIEND I II
HEAVEN GOT A GHETTO
Renta
GORILLAZ IN THE BAY **I II III IV**
TEARS OF A GANGSTA I II
3X KRAZY I II
STRAIGHT BEAST MODE
DE'KARI
TRIGGADALE I II III
MURDAROBER WAS THE CASE
Elijah R. Freeman

Romell Tukes

GOD BLESS THE TRAPPERS I, II, III
THESE SCANDALOUS STREETS I, II, III
FEAR MY GANGSTA I, II, III IV, V
THESE STREETS DON'T LOVE NOBODY I, II
BURY ME A G I, II, III, IV, V
A GANGSTA'S EMPIRE I, II, III, IV
THE DOPEMAN'S BODYGAURD I II
THE REALEST KILLAZ I II III
THE LAST OF THE OGS I II III

Tranay Adams

THE STREETS ARE CALLING

Duquie Wilson

MARRIED TO A BOSS I II III

By Destiny Skai & Chris Green

KINGZ OF THE GAME I II III IV V VI

Playa Ray

SLAUGHTER GANG I II III
RUTHLESS HEART I II III

By Willie Slaughter

FUK SHYT

By Blakk Diamond

DON'T F#CK WITH MY HEART I II

By Linnea

ADDICTED TO THE DRAMA I II III
IN THE ARM OF HIS BOSS II

By Jamila

YAYO I II III IV
A SHOOTER'S AMBITION I II
BRED IN THE GAME

By S. Allen

Coke Girlz

TRAP GOD I II III
RICH $AVAGE
MONEY IN THE GRAVE I II III
By Martell Troublesome Bolden
FOREVER GANGSTA
GLOCKS ON SATIN SHEETS I II
By Adrian Dulan
TOE TAGZ I II III IV
LEVELS TO THIS SHYT I II
By Ah'Million
KINGPIN DREAMS I II III
By Paper Boi Rari
CONFESSIONS OF A GANGSTA I II III IV
CONFESSIONS OF A JACKBOY I II
By Nicholas Lock
I'M NOTHING WITHOUT HIS LOVE
SINS OF A THUG
TO THE THUG I LOVED BEFORE
A GANGSTA SAVED XMAS
IN A HUSTLER I TRUST
By Monet Dragun
CAUGHT UP IN THE LIFE I II III
THE STREETS NEVER LET GO
By Robert Baptiste
NEW TO THE GAME I II III
MONEY, MURDER & MEMORIES I II III
By **Malik D. Rice**
LIFE OF A SAVAGE I II III
A GANGSTA'S QUR'AN I II III IV
MURDA SEASON I II III

Romell Tukes

GANGLAND CARTEL I II III
CHI'RAQ GANGSTAS I II III
KILLERS ON ELM STREET I II III
JACK BOYZ N DA BRONX I II III
A DOPEBOY'S DREAM I II III
JACK BOYS VS DOPE BOYS
COKE GIRLZ
By Romell Tukes
LOYALTY AIN'T PROMISED I II
By Keith Williams
QUIET MONEY I II III
THUG LIFE I II III
EXTENDED CLIP I II
By **Trai'Quan**
THE STREETS MADE ME I II III
By **Larry D. Wright**
THE ULTIMATE SACRIFICE I, II, III, IV, V, VI
KHADIFI
IF YOU CROSS ME ONCE
ANGEL I II
IN THE BLINK OF AN EYE
By **Anthony Fields**
THE LIFE OF A HOOD STAR
By Ca$h & Rashia Wilson
THE STREETS WILL NEVER CLOSE I II
By K'ajji
CREAM I II
THE STREETS WILL TALK
By Yolanda Moore
NIGHTMARES OF A HUSTLA I II III

Coke Girlz

By King Dream
CONCRETE KILLA I II
VICIOUS LOYALTY
By Kingpen
HARD AND RUTHLESS I II
MOB TOWN 251
THE BILLIONAIRE BENTLEYS I II III
By Von Diesel
GHOST MOB
Stilloan Robinson
MOB TIES I II III IV V
By SayNoMore
BODYMORE MURDERLAND I II III
By Delmont Player
FOR THE LOVE OF A BOSS
By C. D. Blue
MOBBED UP I II III IV
THE BRICK MAN I II III
THE COCAINE PRINCESS I II
By King Rio
KILLA KOUNTY I II III
By Khufu
MONEY GAME I II
By Smoove Dolla
A GANGSTA'S KARMA I II
By FLAME
KING OF THE TRENCHES I II
by **GHOST & TRANAY ADAMS**
QUEEN OF THE ZOO
By **Black Migo**

Romell Tukes

GRIMEY WAYS
By Ray Vinci
XMAS WITH AN ATL SHOOTER
By Ca$h & Destiny Skai
KING KILLA
By Vincent "Vitto" Holloway
BETRAYAL OF A THUG
By Fre$h

Coke Girlz

BOOKS BY LDP'S CEO, CA$H

TRUST IN NO MAN
TRUST IN NO MAN 2
TRUST IN NO MAN 3
BONDED BY BLOOD
SHORTY GOT A THUG
THUGS CRY
THUGS CRY 2
THUGS CRY 3
TRUST NO BITCH
TRUST NO BITCH 2
TRUST NO BITCH 3
TIL MY CASKET DROPS
RESTRAINING ORDER
RESTRAINING ORDER 2
IN LOVE WITH A CONVICT
LIFE OF A HOOD STAR
XMAS WITH AN ATL SHOOTER

CPSIA information can be obtained
at www.ICGtesting.com
Printed in the USA
LVHW022233210522
719400LV00013B/725